ASK FOR LOIS

ASK FOR LOIS

JOHN BARCLAY

CUTTING EDGE

ISBN-13: 978-1-970848-14-4

Published by
Cutting Edge Books
PO Box 8212
Calabasas, CA 91372
www.cuttingedgebooks.com

CHAPTER ONE

A long the fifteen-block Sunset Strip in Los Angeles there are more than a score of bistros like the Boomerang Club: dark cafés where you sit at small candlelit tables in lighting that is very kind to the faces of aging ingénues and actors with toupees. Like most of them, the Boomerang features a piano player who plays *My Funny Valentine* at least once a night as a request, and a shapely singer with big breasts, big lungs and small talent. The waitresses in these places are often prettier than the singer, and some of them make more money dating men who come to the clubs than they do on tips and salary.

Each of these places has its special following among the employed and unemployed actors, directors, technicians, and assorted Hollywood insomniacs who come there to unwind, to make fresh contacts, and to bolster their sagging amours. The Boomerang was no better and no worse than most of the other clubs. What made it different was that nearly all the attractive waitresses who worked there were also call girls. In a pinch, any visiting fireman could be taken there and his playmate problem was solved.

On this particular night, the Boomerang was crowded as usual as closing time approached, and many of the customers had begun to leave even before the last appearance of the featured singer, a bosomy creature named Binnie Jones.

A shapely, dark-eyed waitress in a skimpy costume moved among the forest of tables to the bar, aware of the admiring eyes feasting upon her. There was much to feast upon, thanks to her costume. She wore the club's waitress uniform, a tight red outfit resembling a one-piece strapless bathing suit, cut low in front for obvious reasons, black net stockings, and high heels. Long net gloves completed the costume.

She had medium-length brown hair, framing a face that made you take a second look at the pert nose, the high cheekbones, the full red lips, the gray-green eyes that held imprisoned within them a magic feline quality. But Lois Cramer was well aware that her admirers were not looking at her face.

At first, the stares had bothered her. She felt like a schoolgirl mistakenly placed on a burlesque runway and told to perform. While other girls moved with practiced abandon among the white tablesclothed tables with their flickering candles, she felt nervous. The hungry look in a man's eyes as she served him his drink made her feel naked. It seemed they all had X-ray eyes and she was naked before strangers.

Now, after a month, it didn't bother her at all. She had a good figure—as her boss Marty often told her—and she was proud of it. Besides, that's what the stags came to the Boomerang Club for—to stare at the waitresses' long curved legs and into the valley of her bosom and at her rear, across which the costume was pulled so tight it seemed to be sprayed on.

As she watched, she saw a waitress writing something on a matchbook cover, which the girl then gave to a guest sitting at a nearby table. She didn't need to hear their conversation to know what had happened. The guest had been clued in by Marty to ask her for a sex date if he wanted one, and the girl had readily scribbled her address for him. Lois knew that she herself was one of the few holdouts at the Boomerang. Nearly every other girl doubled as a call girl under the boss' protection and for his benefit.

Lois knew about the other girls but she didn't care. What they did was their business. She considered herself a cut above them, someone with talent and a future. Thus, she could afford to ignore her present surroundings, neither approving nor condemning the other girls' way of life.

She stopped at the bar, between the chromium rails that closed off that section from customers.

"Four vodkas on the rocks, Dominick," she said.

"Sure thing, Lois," the bartender said, and his homely face flashed in a smile.

Lois Cramer turned to look at the club. For a weekday night, there was a large crowd. It hadn't happened yet, but one of these nights there was going to be a big producer out there who would notice her. Waiting on tables was unromantic, but at least it got you near show business people on their time off. Besides, there was a certain glamour to working in this environment that appealed to her.

In the daytime the room was a graveyard of empty tables with tablecloths for shrouds, the skeleton monument of stacked chairs to one side, out of the way of the cleaning women who exorcised the ghosts of the previous night. The piano was silent, the multicolored spotlight rested in the glare of the sun streaming warmly through the windows.

But at night it took on a mystical quality. There was the tinkle of glasses, the sound of laughter mingling with the music in the darkened room. A hundred flickering candles, each softened by a translucent cylinder, stood on a hundred tables. The indirect lighting behind the bar silhouetted Dominick and made him a creature of mystery. The spotlight that changed from blue, to red, to green, splashed across Johnny Kay, who, his long brown hair falling across his forehead, an intense look on his lean face, was coaxing gentle standards from the keyboard.

"Lois," a strong masculine voice said beside her, "how's it going, kid?"

She turned to see her boss Marty Masters. The broad-shouldered cabaret owner was immaculately dressed, as usual, and smoothly shaven except for the thin, neatly trimmed mustache. He ran a hand across his thinning black hair in a distracted manner, and she noticed that he was sweating profusely, a sign that he had trouble.

"Not bad, Marty. Something wrong?"

Marty scowled and jerked his head toward the piano. "I'm getting tired of Binnie's tantrums. Ever since she got that write-up in one of the columns she's been impossible. She's forgotten *I'm* the guy who got the story in for her."

Lois looked in the direction of the piano as a white spotlight came on, centering on a tall redhead in a very tight, glittering-blue, sequined gown that showed lots of cleavage. A heavy round of applause came from the tables, and the redhead smiled coolly and acknowledged the ovation with the slightest nod of her pretty head.

"Look at her," Marty said, annoyed. "They give her a polite hand and she acts like she's the Queen of France!"

It was unusual to see the normally calm Marty with his feathers ruffled, but his disenchantment with Binnie didn't interest Lois. She turned back toward the bar, looking up again as Marty touched her arm.

"Lois," he said, his face serious, "you know that could be *your* spot up there, if you wanted it."

Yes, if I also wanted to take Binnie's spot in your bed, she thought. You didn't get anything for nothing from Marty Masters. It was total surrender or go peddle your papers elsewhere.

"What do you say, Lois?" Marty persisted. "Two hundred a week. Your own wardrobe. A new car—"

"Four vodkas on the rocks," Dominick announced behind her.

Lois breathed a sigh of relief. "I'd better get these drinks, Marty. They're for the party in back," she said, nervously but placatingly.

Marty's anger was easily aroused. She couldn't afford to bruise him; she needed the job, and the money it gave her to pay for dramatic lessons, singing instruction and publicity photographs.

"How about dinner after work?" he said pleasantly, still trying.

Even his pleasant tone had a note of command in it, she noticed. Speak softly and carry a big stick—that was Marty's policy. He was probably a nice enough guy, but at times he seemed to have a one-track mind.

"I'd love to, Marty," Lois said. "But I have a date."

"Oh? Who is it this time?"

His eyes watched Binnie who was wrestling vocally with a song that was getting the better of her. He was trying to act as though he hardly cared whether she answered him or not, but Lois knew better. She had the urge to tell him to mind his own business and just leave her alone.

"With Barney Schnepf," she said slowly.

He laughed humorlessly. "That two-bit jerk?" he said. "I suppose he's promised you a bit role in a lousy B-movie, and you fell for it. He's been dangling that same old bait to everything with skirts that'll listen to him; the girls sometimes come across, but Barney never does. If you're going to shack up with somebody, do it with a guy who can really help you. Hell, I could get you stuff ten times better, if you'd give me the chance."

"I'm not shacking up with anyone," she said, more hotly than she'd intended. Barney had a table near the piano, and she hoped he wasn't watching her argue with Marty. Her voice turned soft. "Don't get mad, Marty. Give me a rain check on the dinner."

Marty grinned and patted her arm affectionately. "Sure, kid, sure," he said quietly. "Now, you'd better take those drinks to the customers." He glanced at the redheaded singer and made a production out of wincing. "They'll need them before Binnie's through with the massacre. Just remember what I said. *You* could be up there."

She nodded and moved away quickly from his side with her tray of iced vodkas, feeling like a bird released from a strong fist that never hurt but was a constant threat. It was uncanny how she tensed up just being near him. She wondered if it was because she sometimes suspected she was a fool for not accepting his offer of help.

She forced the thought firmly out of her mind and threaded a path among the candlelit tables, catching fragments of conversation from the occupants.

"—so I said to Sam, 'Look baby, you need a lead in your next flick, tell you what—' "

"—so how can you do a decent picture on a budget like that? The goddamned writers alone want to bleed you for five or six g's plus a percentage—"

"—look, I'd love to do the series, but does my agent care? All he wants is ten per cent of my soul, my life's blood, while he just sits back on his fat can and rakes in the loot I get for him—"

Lois went past the piano, where Johnny Kay gave her a brief, tired smile and then returned his gaunt face to hover over the keyboard. *Poor Johnny,* she thought. He always looked as though he'd been pulled out of a sound sleep. She smiled to herself as she thought of how Marty had once described him—"a relaxed Hoagy Carmichael." But Marty had described Johnny in other terms, too, not so complimentary. It wasn't merely lack of sleep, it was also the drinking—and, maybe, the constant frustration of having recording companies slam doors in his face.

Out of the corner of her eye she saw Barney Schnepf signaling to her, but she pretended not to notice. Binnie's thin tones followed her as she wended her way through the dimly lit labyrinth. There was no getting around it; the redhead's voice was mediocre, and Lois knew that *she* could do much better if given the opportunity. She reminded herself again that opportunity had knocked again that evening. Trouble was, if she opened the door, she'd find a bedroom on the other side.

She reached the end of the room where a party was in progress. They'd shoved a half dozen tables together to form a larger one, and about fifteen men and women sat around it drinking and laughing.

"Ah," someone said, "Florence Nightingale has arrived with the ulcer medicine."

Expertly, Lois guided the drinks from the tray and set them on the table. She froze as she felt a hot hand running up her leg. She turned angrily.

"Stop that!" she said in a furious stage whisper that turned several heads. "Keep your hands to yourself!"

The man laughed and slapped her a resounding blow on the rear. "Just being playful, Florence," he told her, and then giggled idiotically.

"Okay, Jack, cut it," a voice at the head of the table said in a flat command. "You could have knocked her over. As it is, you probably gave the poor girl a bruise."

"Aw, come off it, Elliot," the slapper complained, his eyebrows knitting into a frown, "all I did was give her a love tap."

"The hell you did," the man said. His voice became gentle suddenly as he turned to Lois. "Please excuse my friend, miss. He's a stuntman, and he's used to breaking up tables."

The rest of the party guffawed, and the stunt man looked sheepish.

"I'm sorry," he said, "but I find good-looking *derrières* irresistible."

Lois studied her benefactor. He was a man possibly in his thirties, good-looking without being handsome, with closely cropped hair she was sure was prematurely gray. She liked the warm way he was smiling at her, and she wished she could see the color of his eyes.

"That's all right," she said. "I guess I was just surprised. that's all."

"They ought to let you wear football pads when you carry those drinks." He glanced down at her. "Even *I* think you have a good figure."

She blushed, even though she knew he was stating it as a fact and not making a pass. "I—I've got to go," she said.

She hurried away, aware that her cheeks were still flaming. Behind her, she heard a woman say, "Here's to Elliot Jordan, the best TV director in the business."

Elliot laughed, embarrassed. "You're beginning to sound like my press agent, Sally."

And then their voices were lost in the babble of crowd noises and the wispy lyrics emanating from the throat and heaving bosom of Binnie Jones, singer. Lois looked up to see Barney waving impatiently. She wondered if she'd made an impression on Elliot Jordan; sometimes a TV wheel took a liking to an unknown at first sight. She glanced back, but he wasn't looking in her direction, and her gray-green eyes slitted in annoyance.

"I'll bet that pretty little behind of yours hurts," Barney Schnepf said as she drew close. He rubbed the big diamond on his finger and clucked sympathetically. "I saw the way he whacked you."

"It still stings a little," she admitted.

Out of the corner of her eye she saw Johnny looking curiously at her. He generally gave her a ride home, but he was staying an hour later tonight to run over some new numbers and she'd told him she was tired and would grab a bus. She glanced up at the bar and spotted Marty watching her.

"I can leave in about ten minutes," she whispered as she bent over the table. "I'll meet you in front of the drugstore two blocks down Sunset."

"The drugstore?" Barney repeated, surprised. He was a short, heavy-set man in his fifties with a ribbon of hair combed across his bald head. "The Corvette's out in the parking lot, baby. Save yourself a hike." His pale blue eyes twinkled mischievously and his voice rose and fell in singsong fashion. "After that spanking I should think you couldn't even walk. You must be black and blue."

It hadn't been that hard a slap, but she didn't want to argue about it. "Please, Mr. Schnepf. My boss doesn't approve of my dating customers. Don't make it hard for me."

Schnepf shrugged, held out a ten-dollar bill and got to his feet. "*Mach nichts,*" he said in a bored tone. "So I'll be waiting at the drugstore. Can I get you something maybe? Like rubbing alcohol?"

Lois gave him an annoyed look. Barney's sense of humor was generally not very subtle, but he was still casting director at Acme Artists, and he could open a lot of important doors.

"No, thanks. But I could use a snack. Could we go someplace for a sandwich?"

"Sure," he said. "How about Barney's?"

"If you like," she said uncertainly, "but it's mostly a chile con carne place. I was thinking of a delicatessen."

"And I wasn't thinking of Barney's Beanery, baby," he said with a grin. "I meant Barney Schnepf's place—and that has plenty of delicatessen. We can have ourselves a snack there, and then we can discuss the little part I was telling you about." He glanced with amusement at the bill clutched in her hand. "Keep the change, baby, and buy yourself a night club. See you at the drugstore."

She watched him disappear through the front doors, and then she looked over to the bar where Marty was standing, frowning at her. He shook his head then and turned to other matters.

But it was fifteen minutes before she could leave. When she came out of the dressing room, Johnny was leaning against the wall of the corridor, smoking a cigarette.

"Hi," he said cheerfully. "I thought I'd put in my bid for breakfast. I can stop by when I'm through here and pick you up."

"Thanks, Johnny," she said, trying to turn him down as lightly as she could. "But I'm really very tired."

He grimaced. "Another heavy date?" he said in that tight voice he used when he was annoyed and his feelings were hurt. "When are you going to find time to listen to my songs? I thought you wanted to hear them."

"I do, Johnny," she said. "But not tonight. Let's get together Sunday afternoon."

He shrugged, dismissing the subject. "What did the big bossman want? He offer you that spot of Binnie's again, with all the little strings attached? Have you finally decided to take the plunge?"

She felt the fire mounting into her cheeks, and before it could overflow she turned on her heel and started for the street door.

"Wait a minute, Lois!" he pleaded.

But she refused to listen. It would only lead to the same dismal scene. His moods were mercurial. First, he would apologize abjectly, and then he would hate himself for the apology and become hostile. In the end she knew he would go on to some jam session and dissolve his hurt in a bottle.

It was at times like these that she wanted to take the big boob into her frail feminine hands and shake some sense into him. He had a very real talent, but he insisted on smothering it by feeling sorry for himself and then drowning the sorrow in a sea of alcohol. She could understand it, partly. After a week of accompanying Binnie's tinny voice and of beating down doors at Hollywood recording studios, he was like a kid who had been slapped around so often he'd gotten to expect it. Sometimes, *she* got discouraged from the constant round of agencies and studios that never seemed to have a yes for an answer.

The look on his old-young man's face triggered a wave of pity and she said, "Tomorrow afternoon, then. I really would like to hear the songs, you know that, Johnny."

"Don't strain yourself," he said testily. He made a theatrical bow. "You must excuse me. My public awaits the poor man's George Shearing."

He walked past her and back into the restaurant. Then she ducked out the side door and walked rapidly toward the drugstore, trying not to think of Johnny or Marty or anything except that Barney Schnepf was waiting for her and that he could get her a part in a new musical, *Waltz Me Around*.

Barney's red Corvette, gleaming like a jelly apple in the bright neon of the store window, was waiting with the door open and Barney beside it ready to slam it shut after her.

"I'm sorry I'm late," she said, "but—"

"You're worth waiting for, baby," he said. "Besides, I told you you couldn't walk. And just to show you how much I care, here's a little present." With a flourish, he extended a small bottle of baby oil from his coat and presented it to her, chuckling. "For tender bottoms!"

"Thanks," she said, laughing in spite of herself. Maybe she had him all wrong. It was funny—the baby oil. Nevertheless, she didn't want to go to his place, so she said, "Barney, I'm beat. Could we go to Cantor's or some snack bar for a sandwich. It's simpler, and we could talk about the picture."

"Sure, baby, sure," he said, good-naturedly. "Anything you say. Just hop in. I know a place a few blocks from here."

She felt relieved. He might insist on a good-night kiss, but apparently he wasn't going to try anything complicated. Thank heaven everyone in Hollywood wasn't like Marty Masters.

She got in the Corvette, he slammed the door shut behind her and got in the driver's side. A minute later they were accelerating through the early morning traffic of Sunset Boulevard. Lois closed her eyes, leaned back on the soft leather seat and relaxed, feeling the fresh air fill her lungs and ruffle her hair. It felt good to be outside, away from the smoke-filled club with its noisy clatter of glasses and babble of voices and the merciless eyes of the male patrons who mentally undressed and raped her in a glance.

She snapped her eyes open as Barney made a fast turn. She frowned, as she saw that they were climbing up a road leading into the hills above Sunset Boulevard.

"Where are we going?" she asked. She was curious rather than apprehensive, even though she knew Barney lived in another part of town.

"You'll see," he said mysteriously.

They turned along several dimly lit roads that snaked above the neon-lit boulevard, and then he pulled off the road onto a shoulder that looked over the city. The view below was breathtaking, as always. Los Angeles at night glittered like a pocketful of gems scattered across a jeweler's black square.

"My favorite discussion spot," Barney said. "It's quiet, there aren't any distractions, and two people can think and talk clearly."

He felt under the seat and brought up a paper bag. A moment later he offered her a paper cup of bourbon.

"It is beautiful," she said, gazing in awe at the brilliant panorama below.

"It's yours if you want it, baby," Barney said generously, placing an arm casually across the seat in back of her.

Lois tried to down a slight feeling of uneasiness starting to crawl over her. She sipped the whiskey and felt its rawness burning her throat.

"Barney, can you really get me into the picture?"

"If I said it," Barney said downing his drink, "then I can do it. Have faith in old Barney, baby."

"It's not that I don't have faith but—"

"Then show it, baby, show it!"

He put his arm around her shoulder, the other arm reaching out and drawing her close to him. He pressed his lips hard against hers, wetly, and she tried not to flinch. She had expected a pass, but she hadn't expected it here, not like this. But she knew she mustn't offend him, so she tried to return his kiss.

Encouraged by her reaction, Barney slid his hand down to her thigh and squeezed it experimentally. His fingers moved along her leg, and she quickly covered his hand with her own to stop him from going any farther.

"You drive me nuts, baby," he said. "You know that. I swear I go nuts just watching you move across that floor."

His hands came alive again.

"Please, Barney," she pleaded, trying to control his hands.

He was in no mood to stop. His breath was coming hard and short, and she could almost hear the frantic beating of his heart. His eyes were glazed. He cupped one of her breasts, hurting her. His other hand moved expectantly along her leg under the skirt.

"No, Barney," she almost shouted at him, "I don't want to!"

In desperation, she stopped him by digging her nails into the back of his hands. He winced and pulled his hands away, looking at her in hurt and surprise.

Almost immediately, his hands darted again, his fingers directed toward unbuttoning her blouse. When she pulled away, he gripped the cloth at her neckline and it tore. His hand fumbled for her breast.

"Barney, I said no!"

"Come on, Lois baby," Barney said. "Don't give me the virgin schoolgirl bit. What do I have to do, win a raffle?"

"If that's all you were looking for, you shouldn't have asked me out. You could have had almost any other girl in the place. All I do there is wait on tables."

She felt anger boiling inside her and tears of frustration were beginning to sting her eyes. She should have known it would turn out like this.

"Okay, okay," Barney said wearily. "If you want to play games, we'll play games. You're an innocent little lamb and I'm the Shah of Persia!" His voice turned sour. "Baby, let's cut out the Mack Sennett routine. If you don't like getting laid in a car, let's go to my place where we can get cozy."

"Shut your filthy mouth, damn you!" she blurted.

Barney looked at her for a moment and then scratched his head. "I don't dig this, honey. What's with you, anyway?"

Lois was still seething, but she managed to control her voice. "You made a mistake, Barney, that's all. You just picked the wrong girl. If I'd known that's what you wanted I wouldn't have come out with you. Now, please take me home.

Barney grinned at her. "Come off it," he said. "You know you don't get a part in a movie for nothing." Abruptly, he was at her again, cupping her breast with one hand and lifting her skirt above her knees with the other. "I've got something you want, you've got something I want. You scratch my back, I'll scratch yours; it's as simple as that. Come on, relax. You got a lovely pair of breasts there, you know that. Let's see what they look like."

He pulled her in a sudden move toward him and laid open the décolletage of her blouse, then lifted one of her breasts from its brassiere cup and bent to kiss it.

She pushed at him with a strength doubled by anger and hurt, shoving him so hard that he struck his head against the car door. Then she straightened her skirt and buttoned her blouse.

"I told you to take me home, Barney," she said coldly, "and I meant it."

He glared back at her, fingering his scalp where he'd hit his head. "I'm not going to take you anywhere," he said brusquely, anger flaring in his eyes. "If you want to go home, get out and walk."

"I can't walk down these hills in the dark," she said firmly. "You brought me up here, now take me home."

A dark rage was building in him. The thought that any girl could turn him down when he offered such tempting bait was too much for him. "Get out of the car," he ordered. "I'm not running a taxi."

"And I'm not getting out until you take me home," she said adamantly.

"Damn it, I said get out!"

He reached across her and opened the door. When she ignored it, he shoved her roughly and sent her sprawling out of the car and onto the ground. Dazed and hurt, she picked herself up as Barney revved the motor angrily and held the car in place long enough to get in his parting shot.

"Wake up, Shirley Temple!" he yelled derisively. "Or you'll still be slinging hash when you're thirty."

The car leaped forward, scattering dirt and gravel, the motor echoing the driver's anger.

She watched the car's rapid descent until his lights disappeared around the curve below. Then she dusted off her soiled skirt as best she could and began the slow, tortuous trek down to Sunset Boulevard. The path was so dark and so steep she had to brake herself going down. Barney's last taunt burned in her ears as she trudged down the hill.

You'll still be slinging hash when you're thirty!

He had sounded like her stepmother in St. Louis.

You'll wind up selling ribbons in a dime store! Stella had said.

When her real mother died shortly after her sixteenth birthday, Lois' father had let her continue the dramatic coaching and the singing lessons started by her mother. Then her father married Stella, who insisted the lessons be stopped.

"You'll never get anywhere as a singer," the woman had insisted. "You don't have the voice, and you might as well face it before any more money is thrown away. These swindlers will promise you the moon in order to get your money. If you want to learn something, go to business school like I did."

"My teacher said I've got a good chance to sing professionally if I study for another few years," Lois had said.

The arguments were nothing new to her. It annoyed her that her father had sat behind his newspaper in the small, overheated house in Richmond Heights and pretended not to hear.

"Papa, you promised I could continue the lessons," Lois wailed, but he said nothing, only straightened the paper. She turned back to Stella. "I can work nights after I finish high school to pay him."

"Who's going to pay you, and for doing what?" her stepmother had asked derisively. "What could you do? You have no experience, you don't know shorthand and hardly any typing. All you know are those damned movie magazines and *Variety*. Lois, stop wasting your time and your father's hard-earned money. You don't have that kind of a voice. That teacher of yours is just a crook who wants you to support him. To him, you're just another stage-struck teen-ager who's walked into his trap. All of the girls I've seen there are just like you—romantic, fat and sure that life is a picture with Alice Faye."

"I'm trying to diet," Lois screamed at her. "Stop nagging me about it. Papa, tell her to stop or I'll leave and never come back. I swear I will!"

She had been chubby in those days, with her natural curves hidden by fatty tissue, and Stella seemed to take a great delight in pointing this out to her. Usually, after a while, her father would stir and weakly try to smooth things over. But the arguments would only start again in a few days when the time came for the next lesson. Her stepmother was a churchgoing New Englander who hated music and equated overweight with sinfulness and sloth; when she said damn, she meant damn, literally. Thin as a rail herself, she saw all fat people as gluttons and sensualists and needled her stepdaughter relentlessly about her weight.

Lois learned afterwards from a psychology book that her overeating was compensation for her feelings of being unloved and unwanted. Her stepmother's cruelty in reminding her constantly of her pudginess had made her eat all the more.

She had taken the verbal abuse and all the rest of it—the boiled New England dinners that had become routine, Stella's self-righteous opinion of dance music and vocalists. Lois could listen to her records only by keeping them at her friend's house. She had endured it for nearly three years, though God only knew how she could have stayed night after night in her tiny bedroom after dinner listening to her radio turned down so low that she could barely hear it. And for two years she had given up her singing lessons and joined the church choir at her stepmother's insistence.

If Stella had not destroyed the Peggy Lee and Kay Starr records Harry Pruyn had given her for her eighteenth birthday, she might never had left home and gone out to work on her own. It had been the smartest move she had ever made. She missed her father, but other than that she felt no ties. Ultimately, she had started the voice lessons again and, once away from "home", she began to lose weight. She started working as a singer in small places around St. Louis and Kansas City, but the places were not well known and the pay was low. And she had never been able to lick the sense of failure that Stella had given her by insisting she would never get anywhere as a singer.

It was to prove her stepmother wrong that Lois had in desperation quit her job in St. Louis and taken the bus to Hollywood to scrounge for a job in show business. For that same reason, she was working as a waitress in the Boomerang, clutching at straws like Barney Schnepf who promised the moon to get a chance to make her. Still, she had to try. She could never go back to St. Louis and admit failure. It would be like admitting she wasn't a real person ...

Thinking about it now, as she trudged down the steep dark slope, Lois felt more discouraged than ever. She was no closer to getting into show business than when she'd started. Tonight surely settled Barney Schnepf and any chance she had of getting even a small part in his movie. Then she shrugged resignedly, pulled her torn dress together as best she could, and started down the dark road.

Fifteen minutes later, footsore and miserable, she reached a gas station at the foot of the hill and went into the ladies' rest room. The sight of herself in the mirror made her wince. Her hair was mussed, her lipstick was smeared, and the front of her dress was a gaping ruin. She felt like crying, not so much at her appearance or at what had happened, but at *why* it had happened. She'd thought it would be different with Barney, but it was just like with the others.

She didn't have enough money for a cab, and she couldn't take a bus in her condition. Besides, she could use a sympathetic shoulder to lean on right now. She made her way to a nearby phone booth and dialed the number of the Boomerang Club. Dominick answered, and she asked for Johnny Kay.

"Hello," she heard his voice a moment later.

Lois hesitated. He would know she'd lied to him, but it couldn't be helped. "Johnny," she said, "it's Lois. Can—can you pick me up in your car? I'm—"

"Sure," he said happily. "Are you home?"

"No," she said and gave him the address.

He paused briefly, then he said, "I see," in a flat, tight voice. "I'll be there in ten minutes."

The phone clicked abruptly, and for a moment Lois stared at it and then carefully replaced the receiver. Johnny had guessed what had happened, and he had already tried and condemned her for being so naïve. Worse, it was the possibility that he might be right in his judgment that made her feel suddenly very cold.

CHAPTER TWO

Johnny Kay was abnormally silent as he drove her to her apartment in the down-at-the-heels eastern end of Hollywood. His bony face stared modily, lost in thought, at the expanse of Hollywood Boulevard, empty except for an occasional pair of gay boys mincing along in their private worlds. His silence became rapidly intolerable and Lois forced herself to break it.

"Thanks for coming so soon, Johnny," she said, not looking at him.

"You lied to me," he said tonelessly. "All that jazz about being tired. Why the hell didn't you tell me you were going out with Schnepf? I could have warned you to wear a suit of armor."

"It—it came up suddenly," she said, acutely aware of how easy it is for one lie to breed another. "When I was talking to him at the club. He offered me a part."

Johnny grunted. "Part schmart. He wanted to give you part of himself."

"Johnny!"

"If that's what you want, why the hell don't you play ball with Marty? He'll get you show business contacts up the gazoo."

"I didn't come to Hollywood to get couch cast," she retorted. She sighed wearily. "I don't want to argue with you. Please stop nagging. I called you because I was sick and tired of wrestling with Barney and my dress was torn. Don't make it any more difficult for me."

Her voice cracked at the end. Johnny had opened his mouth to say something, then he thought better of it and fell silent. She was grateful for his understanding. He reached over and squeezed her hand suddenly, gently.

"I'm sorry, Lois. I guess I'm beating the drum too hard." He shook his head. "Only sometimes you get so damned naïve I think you're still in diapers, emotionally. What the hell did you expect from a wolf like Barney. He tries to make everything that walks."

She felt tears returning to her eyes, not with anger now but with the secret knowledge that Johnny was right. She should have known about Barney—and probably about the others, too. As they drew up to the brown stucco mudpie she lived in, she began to sob uncontrollably. Johnny parked the car quickly, took her in his arms and kissed her wet cheeks.

"Come on, come on, Lois. I didn't sound that bad. Don't pay attention. You know me, I'm just a sourball. Especially at this time of night."

She didn't move from the comfortable security of his arms. She shook her head. "It's not that, Johnny. It's just me. This is the third time this week I went out with someone in the industry, and they all tried the same thing." She dried her eyes with a Kleenex from her purse. "Never mind. I'm all right now. Would you like to come up and play some of your songs?"

"At three in the morning? The landlady would toss us both out." But he smiled, pleased. "Besides, I left them at the club. But I would like a cup of coffee."

"You'll have it," she said.

They got out of the car, and he took her arm and guided her up the steps.

"Watch your step," she warned. "The landlady still hasn't put a new bulb in that hall light."

They made their way through the dark hallway, Johnny remembering just in time to avoid the third step which was sadly in need of repair. He understood how discouraging it could be for Lois to come home here, because his place was really not much better. He, too, had walls that needed painting and woodwork in need of dusting. As she poked the keyhole with her key, his nostrils flared at the lingering odor of boiled cabbage.

"How I hate that smell," she whispered with a shudder. "It's all the neighbors seem to eat."

She entered her room and clicked the switch beside the door. A shaded light bulb flared overhead. Johnny followed her into the living room and closed the door behind him. She went to the window and pulled down the shade.

"I'd better take this dress off before I tear it any more."

"And while you're doing that, I'll put the coffee on," Johnny volunteered.

As he disappeared into the kitchen, Lois went to a small portable phonograph on a table near the opposite wall and lifted its cover. The record was on the turn-table where she'd left it after rehearsing with it earlier that day. She turned the knob, the record whirled, and a few seconds later the mellow tones of Peggy Lee drifted into the room.

"You're going to wear that record out," Johnny called from the kitchen.

"Then I'll buy another one," she said. "That's how great *I* want to be someday."

She closed her eyes and listened to the soft voice singing the smooth phrases. She mouthed the words, imagining herself in the spotlight at the Boomerang Club with a vast horde of Important People hanging onto every syllable.

Then she opened her eyes. The night club and the legion of admirers had vanished. In their place was the tiny flat with its worn brown carpet and beat-up furniture, fitting surroundings for a mood that even the dulcet tones of Peggy Lee could not dispel.

Within these four walls was her home—and she had little chance of getting a better one until she made good in show business. The spinach-green couch with the frayed cushions was a visual atrocity against the tobacco-colored rug. The scarred end table looked defeated even under the bright yellow cover she had purchased in a vain effort to make the drab place look cheerful. She changed her dress, feeling tired and discouraged.

When she returned to the living room, Johnny was sitting on the couch waiting for her. He had a glass of whiskey in one hand. He picked up its mate from the coffee table and handed it to her. She sat down beside him.

"Why do you do it?" he asked sadly, nodding at the room. "How in God's name can you stomach this week after week?

"Sure," he went on. "Voice coaching, piano rental, dramatic lessons." He shook his head. "I just don't get it, Lois, I honestly don't. I'd be rich if I had a dollar for every one of you crazy kids who drop everything and come out here to break into this business. You're like moths rushing into a flame. They print articles in magazines telling you to stay away. They write books. They do everything but beat you over the head." He sighed. "And still you come out by the busload. And just like the articles say, you get jobs as carhops, waitresses or typewriter punchers while you wait for that big break—or you make it between the sheets if you're like Binnie."

Lois sipped her drink gloomily. Her depression deepened. "If it's going to be another two-dollar lecture, Johnny, you can spare me the details."

Johnny got up from the couch, walked to the piano and sat down. From the phonograph the voice of Peggy Lee massaged the air. Johnny swung around in his seat.

"All I wanted to point out was simply that your approach is all wrong, and if you haven't found it out by now you're pretty naïve. The facts have been under your pert little nose right along, and it's about time you faced them: if you're starting out in this business, either you make it in this town on your back with guys like Marty and his fat-cat chums—or you just don't make it. The way you're trying to do it is just a waste of time—living in a dump like this, begging for auditions from punks who only want to drag you into the bushes and probably couldn't get you a part in a picture if they tried. Look, I know I sound corny but—well, have you considered going back to St. Louis?"

"I'm never going back," Lois snapped. Her gray-green eyes slitted angrily. "I hate the place. Besides, what would I do there, live with my father and my stepmother who doesn't like me? Work in some third-rate joint near Gaslight Square with its imitation Greenwich Village atmosphere? No, thanks."

She flushed darkly and went on, "I borrowed money from an aunt, and I came out here because I swore I'd make it or bust. Okay, so I'm not a Dinah Shore or a Peggy Lee, but I'm a lot better than these simpering tinny-voiced cows they've got here now. My voice has been praised by some of the best coaches in St. Louis. I've won three beauty contests. I've acted in summer stock. I *know* I'm better, and I've got proof of it—in records, clippings, letters from people. What the devil am I supposed to do, sit around in St. Louis and let some horrible mediocrity like Binnie Jones take all the prizes?"

Johnny grunted, unimpressed. "So you put your fistful of clippings from papers nobody ever heard of in a twenty-dollar scrapbook and come out here ready to break down Jerry Wald's door. Don't you know nobody comes out here cold, for Pete's sake?"

"I didn't come out here cold," Lois retorted, beginning to hate him for putting her on the defensive. "I had a letter from a big distributor who told me to take it to studio heads and to agents."

"They turn those out on IBM machines," Johnny said mercilessly. "So what happened? You saw Mr. Big and wouldn't spend the weekend with him in Palm Springs, and he told you to go to hell. Spare *me* the details. I've heard the story before, a hundred times."

"You're wrong. Nothing like that happened. The man I saw got me a couple of small parts, but that was all he could do."

"How small?" Johnny wanted to know.

She wished she could wipe that smirk off his knowing face. "Some—well, some extra work. No lines. I was in a couple of crowd scenes. But at least he tried. He said they couldn't take the chance on giving a large part to an unknown. He told me to try and land something with a smaller, independent producer."

"Sure," Johnny said sarcastically. "And told his secretary to type you another letter." He ran his finger down the piano keys in a disgusted crescendo and got to his feet. "Oh Christ, why don't you wake up. Either get the hell out of Hollywood and lead a normal life or play the angles for all they're worth. If I could get a million record sale—or any sale, for that matter—by sleeping with the wife or even the old maid aunt of the gun who runs Geronimo Records, I'd break the world's track record getting to her bedroom. Idealism and chastity went out with Rebecca of Sunnybrook Farm!"

"You don't mean that," she said. "I've heard you talk about the girls at the club too often. You don't mean a word of what you're saying."

"The hell I don't," Johnny said darkly. "Have you ever seen where those girls live? Have you seen the cars they drive and the clothes they wear? Every time I come up here I feel like scooping you up and taking you someplace where the walls don't look like something out of a Boris Karloff movie and the furniture doesn't make you want to vomit."

"I'll get the coffee," she said coldly, getting up and trying to control her rising anger.

He was in one of his sardonic moods which she hated most, the kind of mood in which he clawed at everything around him, probably in order to still his own sense of insecurity. He'd been drinking between sets at the club, and his face was beginning to get flushed. She wished now she hadn't invited him up.

He followed her into the kitchen and his voice rose to a near shout, dripping with cynicism and bitterness. "What is with you, anyway? What are you so afraid of? Oh, I can understand why you don't want to go to bed with an unknown song writer and half-assed piano player like me. But how come you pass up Marty and the red carpet treatment? The minute you dropped your pants you'd be in Binnie's spot and living like Jayne Mansfield for a change. Think of the beautiful front you could put up, the chance to really display your talent."

"Stop it!" she shouted at him. She'd been listening quietly, closing her eyes and clenching her fists as though that would keep out his words. "If you're going to talk with a dirty mouth I wish you'd go. What I do is my own business, damn you. And if I choose to live this way—"

"Ah, but do you?" he interrupted, smiling. "What's your problem, are you afraid of sex? Certainly you're not a virgin at your age. You've had a guy, haven't you?" His grin grew broader as he saw the flush of red creep into her face, across the high cheekbones. "I thought so."

"You thought what?" she said, annoyed with his smug attitude.

She was astonished and irritated at how swiftly Harry Pruyn had leaped into her mind when Johnny mentioned virginity. That bastard Harry, who had kept her on a string for two months with a promise of marriage and, when she'd invited everyone she knew to the wedding, took off for New York.

"Nothing," Johnny said wearily, his mood veering sharply as it often did when he was half drunk. He stood behind her and placed his hands on her shoulders. "Forget what I said. I guess I'm just jealous of all these phony guys you go out with. Chalk it up to vanity, if you like. There's no percentage in your getting close to me. What good can a broken-down piano player do you? Except make some arrangements for you to sing—and I've done that."

He released her shoulders and she turned within the circle of his arms and kissed him impulsively on the mouth.

"Don't say that, Johnny. You're the only real friend I have. You know I'm grateful."

He looked at her for a moment, his eyes roaming her features, studying the wisp of hair falling across her forehead and the deep gray-green of her eyes, the smooth cheekbones, the pert nose and the rich full lips now parted slightly.

"Lois," he breathed, and she felt his arms tighten about her. "Lois."

He drew her roughly to him and kissed her hard on the mouth, his lips working hungrily against hers. She placed her own arms around his neck, returning his kiss, feeling sorry for him and wanting him to know she really liked him. After a moment, she pulled away and smiled, trying not to show her concern at the tenseness evident in his lean face and the way his eyes were caressing her, not only her face this time but her body confined in the tight wrapper. She could feel his fingers trembling.

"Let's—let's go into the other room," he said, his voice hoarse.

He licked his lips and looked at the thin wrapper covering her. With a sudden movement that startled her, he pulled open her garment and stared hungrily at the firm breasts that spilled over the edges of the bra. He pulled her to him again and buried his face over her shoulder and down toward the valley of her breasts.

"Please, Johnny," she begged.

She pressed her hands flatly against his chest and tried to push him away with all her strength. But she was tired, almost exhausted, from the job and from wrestling with Schnepf and the long walk down the hill, and he blocked her feeble efforts with no difficulty. He half led, half dragged her to the couch in the living room and tried to force her down on it.

"No, Johnny," she begged. "Please don't."

As he kissed her, he forced the wrapper down her shoulders, then yanked the bra upward and her breasts, released, thrust out boldly. His eyes glazed and, for the moment, he seemed hypnotized by the nipples.

Lois, stunned by his sudden exposure of her, seemed incapable of interfering with his purpose. His voice was almost a whine now as his hands kneaded her breasts.

"Look, you don't understand, Lois. I'm crazy about you. Honestly I am, honey. If I didn't have this inter-locutory divorce from Sylvia I'd marry you tomorrow."

Having convinced himself that his intentions were honorable, he began forcing her down on the couch again, his mouth enveloping one of her nipples and a hand tearing at her slip.

Loathing crept into Lois' throat, and she felt as if she was going to vomit. Johnny's frantic pawings reminded her of all the other maulings she'd had to take. On impulse, she swung her open palm in an arc that ended at his cheek. Johnny released her and stepped back, surprised by the blow.

"Is that why you came up here," she accused angrily, "to try and rape me? You saw a near miss and thought you'd finish the job, is that it?"

Johnny held a hand to his stinging cheek. "No, of course not," he protested, "you've got it all wrong." The glazed look had left his eyes to be replaced by one of sadness and helplessness.

She let her wrath flow out, uninhibited. "You're all alike," she blurted. "Bastards, with only one thing on your filthy minds. All that nonsense about wanting to help me!"

"I'm sorry," Johnny said, making a tentative move toward her. "I didn't mean—"

"Just get out of here and leave me alone!" she screamed at him. "I thought you were the one person I could trust—the one man I could talk to without being afraid of getting pawed like a cheap tramp!" Her voice rose higher and higher, the frustrations of the day—and night—welling up into a flood of recriminations. "You're worse than all the others! They, at least, come right out with their propositions, but you—you make like a friend and then jump on me—"

The phone rang suddenly, cutting her off in mid-sentence. Startled, they stared at each other for a moment The phone rang again and Lois, her shoulders sagging, crossed to it and picked it up.

"Hello," she said tentatively.

The landlady's strident voice squawked almost unintelligibly, demanding immediate silence and threatening to call the police.

"But—" Lois managed to stutter.

"I know you've got a man up there," the landlady went on self-righteously. "I could spot you for that kind of girl the minute you walked in, and I'm sorry I rented the place to you. Well, you can just pack your things and move out by the end of the month!"

The phone clicked dead, and Lois stared at it blankly. She replaced the receiver in its cradle, and looked up to see a subdued Johnny Kay standing in the center of the room, his arms held helplessly at his side, looking like a small boy who's been reprimanded.

"Lois—"

She shook her head impatiently. "No, Johnny. Don't say anything. Just go. I've had all I can take in one night. I'll—I'll see you at the club tomorrow."

"Sure," he said.

He paused at the door briefly as though he wanted to say something, then changed his mind and left. She could hear his footsteps shuffling down the hallway, the sound of the car starting, then silence.

The Peggy Lee record had spun to a close and the phonograph had shut itself off automatically. Lois started it up again, turned the sound down to a whisper, poured herself a water glass half full of whiskey, and sat down on the couch. She closed her eyes and listened to the music, sipping slowly at her drink. Softly, she sang the words, not thinking of anything else.

After a while, thanks to the whiskey and the recording, the world became a normal, sane place again. She opened her eyes and looked around the room, her mind clear and seeing things as though for the first time. So she had to move, did she? All right, so she'd move. But where? To some other crummy room that was the twin of this one? Was this to be her life, this and the constant stream of wrestling matches with fourth-rate directors and producers whose only thought was to get her into the sack?

Despite his actions tonight, Johnny was her only friend, and she felt sorry for him as she recalled the beaten, bewildered look on his face when she'd ordered him out. If she had to take all these pawings, even from a friend, why not take them deliberately, in the interests of her career?

The answer had been there all the time—right in front of her blind, gray-green eyes—and she'd been a fool for not seeing it. It wasn't too late. In the morning she'd start doing the smart things, the things you had to do to get ahead in this lousy world.

And the first thing she had to do was call Marty Masters!

CHAPTER THREE

"Masters speaking," Marty's voice came over the telephone, crisp, businesslike.

She hesitated. "This is Lois, Marty."

"Oh, hello, Lois," he said. His voice sounded friendly now, but also wary. "Anything wrong?"

"No. I just wondered. Could I come over and see you today, maybe this afternoon—that is, if you're not too busy?"

"Never too busy to see you, kid," Marty said affably. "What did you have in mind?"

"What we talked about last night."

"Oh." He thought for a moment, and she found herself hoping he hadn't gotten sore at her and changed his mind. There were a lot of other girls Marty could help who wouldn't give him such a hard time. "Have you had breakfast or lunch yet?"

"No."

"Good. Come over now and have brunch with me. You've never seen my pad. I got a great view. You'll love it."

"You're sure you're not too busy?"

"Not if you're coming to discuss what we talked about last night. It's a wise decision, by the way. Oh, and bring your swim suit along. Looks like it's going to be a scorcher."

"All right, Marty. By the way, what's the nearest street at the bottom of your hill. I think I'd better walk up. My car won't make it."

He laughed. "I'm surprised that wreck can even make it around the corner. Don't worry, we'll get you a good car; tomorrow we can go shopping for one—a brand-new T-bird, maybe. Meanwhile, just take a cab and I'll settle when it gets here. Okay, kid?"

He sounded happy, and she was pleased that his mood was infecting her. "Okay, Marty."

When Lois hung up, she was aware that her heart was beating wildly. But the decision had been made, and she would follow it through. She took a shower and selected her best dress from the closet, the one she wore to interviews. In a sense, she was going to an audition, an important one that could change her life and really get her started on a career in show business. So she applied her make-up with great care, shaping out the full lips with precision, curving the eyebrow line just so.

But her heart didn't stop its frantic beating and by the time her cab drew up to Marty's house forty minutes later, it was pounding with an incessant, ever-increasing rhythm. For a moment after the cab stopped, she sat in the cab and looked at the big, sprawling house.

The driver turned and said, "This is the right address, lady, isn't it?"

The sound of his voice stirred Lois into action. Impulsively she opened her purse, took out some bills and handed them to him. It made her feel better to pay for the cab herself. She got out, walked up the concrete steps ribboning a carpet of green ground vines, pressed the doorbell firmly. She listened to the chimes echoing inside the house, and she waited, tightening her grip on the beachbag in her hand.

Marty came to the door in an expensive robe of foulard silk covering silk heliotrope pajamas. He was cleanly shaved, except for the hairline mustache, and his straight black hair was neatly

combed back. His welcoming smile made her feel more nervous than relaxed. She imagined it was a thinly disguised leer of
triumph.

His tone seemed sincere. "I'm glad you came, kid," he said
when the door was closed. "Come on, I'll show you the dump
while Ramon is fixing us brunch. The fifty-cent tour."

He led her through several expensively furnished rooms carpeted with a heliotrope wall-to-wall material that felt like turf
under her feet.

"Chenille weave," he said proudly, sensing her appreciation.
He fondled the big diamond on his finger and smiled at her.
"The most expensive wall-to-wall carpeting you can get. Feels
like walking on air. And how about that furniture? All picked by
one of the best interior decorators in town, same guy who does
the homes of the big TV stars. Take a good look, kid. If you like
anything, I can have it sent over to your place—your *new* place, I
mean. I got an apartment picked we can take a look at later, just
above the Strip, not far from here."

He motioned her on through the rooms, and Lois followed
him in growing wonder. The night club owner got an almost
childlike delight in showing her the place, and despite her tenseness she could not help being excited by everything. It was the
sort of place she'd pictured whenever she thought of herself as a
famous movie and TV star. The cantilevered house was perched
on the edge of the canyon, and the view from the veranda was
impressive. On one side she could see the peaks of the Santa
Susanna Mountains and on the other the Pacific Ocean.

Marty took her by the hand and led her into a huge master bedroom with high ceilings and the largest bed she had ever
seen. It was the kind of bed you could imagine a Sultan in, complete with harem. Beside it was a night stand with a modern
lamp and a telephone. At the foot of the bed was a marble-topped

coffee table. Beyond, covering most of one wall, French windows opened to a magnificent vista that included the distant ocean. It was breath-taking.

"This is where we eat," Marty said, smiling. "Can you think of a better place to enjoy food?"

"But there isn't enough room on this veranda," Lois said.

A young Filipino in a white jacket wheeled in a trolley laden with covered dishes. He transferred the dishes and a coffee pot to the marble table and then left as quietly as he had come.

"Does that answer your question?" Marty doffed his robe, dropped it casually into a nearby chair. "Breakfast in bed, kid, how's that for sheer luxury? I got the idea reading Winston Churchill. Did you know he used to stay in bed for hours reading his mail, talking to assistants, and even making trans-Atlantic phone calls? The minute I read that I said, 'Marty, that's for you!' "

He stopped and watched her face. "I've got a lovely pair of pajamas, your size, in the dressing room to the right there."

Lois felt the color creeping into her cheeks.

"Anything wrong, kid?" he asked softly. "You like breakfast in bed, don't you? Everybody does, if they can get it."

When she still did not move, he said, "You look a little beat. Tell you what, why don't you take a quick bath in some perfumed suds. That'll tone you up. I'll just have a coffee and read my mail. Okay?"

She nodded, grateful for the extra time to get adjusted. She entered the adjoining room, selected a pair of knee-length heliotrope silk pajamas and went on into the bathroom. It was done in heliotrope tiles, of course, and had a sunken tub. She smiled to see the bubble bath was heliotrope in color.

Marty was right. The pink suds caressed her naked body and relaxed her, and in a subtle but very real way it also made her feel more at home. Thoughts of her waitress work and the apartment she lived in were very far away. She lay back and closed her eyes, enjoying the luxurious warmth and scent of the suds.

When she opened her eyes a moment later, she saw her wet, nude body in a mirror on the opposite wall. The sight of her nakedness altered her mood and made her frown worriedly. There were few men who had seen her completely undressed, and certainly no strangers. Yet in a few minutes Marty would see her that way. Perhaps she was a fool for coming here like this—for jumping into bed with her boss. Calling him had been a momentary aberration. Going to bed with him would be insane. She stared moodily at her reflection. There was still time to get out of it. She could tell him she'd changed her mind.

It might be messy and he might get angry, but that might be preferable to being his mistress. The idea of his having that kind of hold on her, of his being able to treat her as though she was merchandise he was getting on credit, made her wince. She had managed to stave Marty off just as she had the others. If she allowed him to make love to her, her whole status would change, she would never be the same again.

She leaned back uncomfortably, her breasts half submerged, looking as if they were floating, the pink nipples thrusting up above the waterline like tiny snorkels. Her eyes swept downward to her flat belly, to the sleek thighs, the V of their juncture.

She shuddered.

His hands would soon be running over her hotly, invading, probing, insisting on taking what would later be paid for.

She sat up straight, perspiration beading her brow, panic gnawing at the decision she had made so boldly and so recently.

What in heaven's name am I doing here? she asked herself, horrified, *Just because I had to fight off a cheap wolf and had a fight with my landlady, I run up here and go to bed with my boss. I must be out of my mind.*

With jerky, frantic movements, she got out of the tub and rubbed her skin with a Turkish towel until it glowed pink. She had decided.

I can't go through with it, she told her mirrored self silently. *I can't. I'm not a girl who just sleeps around, and I'll tell Marty that. I'll tell him I was fed up with my job and with Barney and the dump I live in and the bitch who kicked me out, and I couldn't think straight.*

But a moment later she was no longer sure. She thought of Johnny's words about working in a drive-in and crawling back to her stepmother.

"You'll never get anywhere as a singer. You don't have the voice, and you may as well face it!"

She felt her temples throb as Stella's words returned to taunt her, and unconsciously she clenched her fists in defiance. She closed her eyes. *Oh God, if I only had time to think.*

But that was one thing she didn't have—time. If she didn't go through with it now, Marty might not give her another chance. She opened her eyes and stared at herself in the mirror, at the woman's body, firm, full, desirable. But how would it be in a few years? Would age cause the breasts to sag, the stomach to go to pot?

Damn it! she cried silently at the mirror. *This is no time to quit, not when you're so close. It's a move you've been leaning toward for months, and it's the only way if you ever hope to succeed. So stop playing Joan of Arc and do it!*

Suddenly she heard Marty's voice say, "Honey, food's going to get cold. Don't take too long."

She looked up, startled, then realized his voice had come from a speaker beside the tub.

When she entered the bedroom a few minutes later, Marty was already propped up in bed and having coffee from a cup on his night table. He smiled and patted the bed beside him.

Lois had made up her mind there would be no hesitation. She pulled back the silk coverlet and got in under it beside him. It was then she discovered he was wearing only the top of his pajamas. He put his arm around her and kissed her, and she felt another, quick flash of panic, but he turned away from her and pressed a button on the night table. Immediately, the marble coffee table slid over the top of the bed and stopped when it reached them.

Marty chuckled at the look of surprise on her face. "I know an electronics executive in town who dreamed up one of these for his place at the beach. I asked him to build one for me." He nodded. "Nice guy—for an egg-head. Met him at a poker party."

He busied himself uncovering dishes on the table. Breakfast was the fanciest Lois had ever had. Beside the Canadian bacon and eggs, there was fresh papaya, guava jelly, pâté de foie gras from Strasbourg, and English crumpets. It was evident that Marty liked to live well.

He leaned over and kissed her again, casually, and then returned to his food.

"Now then, we've got to get you started on your new career in show business. First of all, I'm taking over completely. Just send me all the bills. Don't worry, we'll call it a loan or an advance— I'll even have some papers drawn up to that effect, and we'll have the contracts in my office tomorrow for you to sign."

He chewed thoughtfully, organizing his thoughts. "Today, we'll go take a look at your new place, and then we can go see a car dealer I know. He just got in some new T-birds, and you can pick out one you like. I'll open up some charge accounts around town, and if you like some particular store I don't know you can have them call me. I'll fix it."

Lois was so overwhelmed she could hardly eat. She was thinking of how much longer she could have gone on knocking at unresponsive doors. Marty went on, expansively describing all the things he would arrange, including acting roles in TV and movies and singing in Binnie's spot.

It was this step that excited Lois most. She knew that as the featured singer at the Boomerang Club she would be seen by scores of TV and movie directors and producers. People like Elliot Jordan, for instance, who saw her now only as a waitress with shapely hips. Hearing her sing, seeing her by the piano in a good dress and with the proper lighting would make all the difference in the world. She listened quietly as he talked, staring out at the sea and the horizon but seeing instead the career that had eluded her and was now so very close.

Marty wiped his lips with a napkin and pressed the button on the night table. The marble coffee table retreated down the length of the bed and stopped. Marty looked at her and smiled.

Lois tried to smile back at him, but somehow her face muscles refused to co-operate. She felt her heartbeat increase its tempo. She felt cold and sought words that would delay the inevitable, but no words came. She had a sudden absurd impulse to leap out of bed and run as fast as she could.

"Something wrong, kid?" Marty's voice was gentle, soothing, concerned.

She looked at his smooth, pale cheeks and the thin mustache and shook her head. Satisfied, he reached out and pulled her close, cupping her breasts and kissing them. She had thought his love-making would be rough but, instead she detected a detachment, almost as if it were a routine, like a master fondling a pet, possessively and with a sense of ownership. She cringed.

His hand began to explore the curves of her body in a practiced manner, as his lips teased her nipples and, in a moment, despite herself, she felt her body responding. There was immediate resentment to this response, until his muscular body began to dominate hers completely. There was no tenderness in his love-making, only a great deal of finesse and self-assurance. His fingers played deftly with her breasts and thighs, like a musician's playing an instrument, and she tried to let herself go completely, hoping to get lost in sensation.

But he was in no hurry. He smiled at her, knowing that she was his and his alone, whenever he wanted her, and the thought pleased him. After a moment of caressing her he would ease up for a while and then slowly begin again, arousing himself out of his matter-of-factness to a higher and higher pitch of excitement each time.

As his fingers moved closer and closer, up her inner thighs, she closed her eyes and concentrated on the changes that would come to her life. First of all there would be a chance to be a featured singer at the Boomerang, and that was the most wonderful thing of all. People would know she was a singer and not just a tray carrier with a sexy build. Her name would be featured on the marquee, there would be releases about her sent to *Variety* and *The Hollywood Reporter* and all the L.A. newspapers.

Marty was pressing forward with new aggression now, his mouth hot on hers, moving from side to side, wet and insistent, his tongue plunging deep, invading boldly and relentlessly. Lois moaned once when his hand became more venturesome and Marty, thinking she was at last responding, murmured, "Atta baby ..."

She thought of the old apartment she would never have to spend another night in, and the new apartment above the Strip that was waiting for her. She thought of the new T-bird she'd have, maybe as soon as this afternoon. She made herself relax and she envisioned the club, the expensive, clinging gown, with the spotlight on her and the eyes of the audience drinking it all in.

The picture in her mind was so real, so vivid that Marty's caresses almost felt as though they were happening to someone else. She stayed with her audience at the club while Marty, his matter-of-factness completely gone now, wheezed with passion, his maleness pressing forward, his hands cruelly thrusting her thighs apart.

Still on the dais at the club, she sang to her appreciative audience, phrasing the way Peggy Lee did and then going her one better.

Marty's plunging rhythm became more insistent and, momentarily, she brought herself back to the present, simulating passion, determined to make him believe he was getting what he wanted—response.

She could feel his arms tightening around her, pulling her closer to him, but she was thinking of what it would be like to get offers from the top directors in Hollywood, men like Otto Preminger and Anatole Litvak who would turn to her if they needed an actress who could also sing, or someone like Elliot Jordan in TV.

She saw herself getting an offer to be a featured singer in a class A dramatic series, like Connie Stevens in *Hawaiian Eye*. Then when she was much better known as a singer, she'd have her own show like Dinah Shore and she'd be invited back regularly to the Copa in New York, the Pump Room in Chicago, the Crescendo on the Strip, the top spots in Las Vegas.

In her state of exaltation it all seemed not only possible but likely. And what Marty was doing to her, his breath now coming in short, quick gulps, became unimportant, a cold-blooded proposition, a means to an end.

When it was over, as she lay beside him, Lois felt relieved that she had been able to go through with it. An instant later, she worried about something else. Had Marty noticed any revulsion on her part, any holding back as he made love to her? Had he been aware of her shrinking inwardly as he pressed her body close to him?

There had been a moment when she had even felt nauseous as she vaguely heard his animal-like grunts, his viselike grip, and the final, tremendous shudder.

Now that it was over and she lay stretched out beside him, her flesh feverish and damp from his love-making, the nausea returned and she was afraid of shrinking away from him if he touched her now or wanted to make love to her once more. She prayed inwardly that he would not want her again right away. She wasn't sure she could fake it again, and if he noticed her coolness it would only displease him.

Marty leaned back contentedly in the bed and stared thoughtfully at the ceiling. "Can you fill in for Binnie in a few days, or do you want more time to rehearse? I'll need a few days to do some good promotion in the trade papers and the regular dailies. I want to give you the whole build-up."

Lois breathed a sigh of relief. For one horrible moment she had wondered what would happen if Marty was not pleased with her. But that was past, and everything would be all right now.

"I can go on whenever you say," she told him. "I've been practicing the numbers at home—just in case." She frowned. "But what about Binnie?"

Marty laughed and kissed her. "Don't worry your pretty head about Binnie." He glanced at his wrist watch. "Why don't you take a dip in the pool and a sunbathe for a half-hour while I make some business calls."

Lois nodded. Marty had made the statement as a request, but she recognized the authoritative undertones. She was pleased that it didn't bother her.

Marty waited until she was out of the room, then he reached for the phone and dialed a number in Bakersfield.

"Jim Fritch?" he said a moment later. "Marty Masters in L.A. Where the hell've you been keeping yourself? You haven't been down in weeks. What about the oil drilling deal we talked about?"

He waited tensely for the other man's reply. Jim Fritch had options on some of the richest oil fields in California. Anybody he allowed to finance his operations usually doubled and sometimes tripled the investment in six months.

"I'll have to think about it some more, Marty," Jim said. "I've been avoiding L.A. and going up to San Francisco. More night life and prettier girls."

It was the opening Marty had been waiting for. "Wait till you see the kid I've got for you here," he said. "You never saw anything so lovely in your life."

"No kidding," Fritch said, interested. "What's she like?"

"Brunette. Green eyes. Curves that don't quit, and a pair of jugs you can spot a block away. A doll in every department."

"Has she got a face?"

Marty grunted. "Has Liz Taylor got a face? I said she's a doll in every department, and I meant it. Maybe you can use her in that picture you're always talking about."

"I'm not making a picture, and you know it. That's just talk."

"Okay, so who cares. The important thing is, you *might* make a picture, and this kid is movie-struck, but good. You know the type. Eats and sleeps show biz. Spends all her time and dough going to agents, taking drama and voice lessons."

"Sounds possible," the oilman said. "She one of your regular girls?"

"That's the great thing, she's not a call girl," Marty said. "A friend of mine, practically a virgin. I tell you, Jim, this kid's got class, and if she thought you might have a big part in a picture for her ..." He let his voice trail off meaningfully. "Are you interested?"

He heard Fritch chuckling. "You're a corrupt bastard, Masters. I'd hate to have my kid sister working in that high-class cathouse you run. You know damn well I'm interested. Anyway, I'd like to come down there and take a look at her, maybe in a week or two, after I get back from New York What's this sexpot's name?"

"She's my new singer," Marty said, triumphantly. "You can see her at the club. Just ask for Lois."

CHAPTER FOUR

Marty pulled his car to a stop in front of Lois' apartment building and sat looking at it for a moment. "You know," he said, "this dump reminds me of a place I lived in once back in New York."

When he saw her living room a moment later, he said, "My God, what is this, Early Hitchcock? When do the vampires come out of the walls? Don't tell me you can't do better than this on what you make at the club?"

"I have a lot of expenses," she said defensively. "Voice lessons, payments on the car, money I owe my aunt back home—"

"Sorry, kid," Marty said. "Forget it. Anyway, your pioneering days in the West are finished. Where's your suitcase? The sooner we get out of here the better. And don't take those crummy dresses. We'll get new ones."

She got the worn leather bag from behind the bed and started shoveling things into it—her make-up, photographs of her parents, personal papers.

He picked up her suitcase a few minutes later and walked to the door. Lois hesitated, looking around her at the drab room, with the huge out-of-place piano dominating it. She thought of all the times she had looked around the room and sworn to herself that this was just a temporary measure until she got started in show business.

They drove to a Ford dealer on Wilshire Boulevard, and Marty took her by the hand and led her into the showroom where he nodded to a man who smiled and pointed to a light pink Thunderbird on the floor.

"Well," Marty said, "how do you like it?"

"Marty, it's—it's beautiful," she said, meaning it.

It was sparkling new, the loveliest car she had ever seen in her life, luxurious but looking like it could go as fast as anything on the road. It was the kind of car she'd always wanted but could never afford.

"Glad you like it, kid," he said. "It'll be delivered to your place this afternoon."

"But, Marty—I can't afford a car like this."

"You can if I write out the check," Marty said with a chuckle.

"And I can't accept it as a present, either," she said determinedly. "I appreciate the gesture, Marty, but I just can't."

Marty laughed. "Don't be silly, kid. Who said anything about me giving it to you as a present? You need a decent car to get around in, so I'm loaning you the money so you can buy one."

"But such an expensive one. Couldn't I get a regular Ford, so I'd at least have a chance to pay you back?"

Marty shook his head. "You've got to learn to think big and act big. You're stepping up in the world and you've got to let people know it. You've got to act the part. A pink T-bird is just another show business prop, like the apartment and the gowns you'll wear when you're singing. It all helps to impress the people we want to impress. You've got a lot of class, kid, and we've got to shout it out to the world every way we can."

"All right, Marty," she said. "But I want to pay you back."

"Great. We'll draw up the papers tomorrow in my office and make it all legal. I'll be giving you a loan, and you'll be paying it back out of your earnings. Everything businesslike."

Marty made out a check to the dealer and told the man to deliver the car to Lois' new address.

Lois could feel the excitement flowing through her again as they entered the lobby of the Sunset Paradise a short time later. An expensive new apartment building just above the Sunset Strip, the place was a study in tropical landscaping, with a lagoon-like pool that was the largest Lois had ever seen.

Her new apartment was on the top floor, with a view of the city below. The living room was carpeted with soft, thick material into which her feet sank. Ceiling to floor drapes covered one wall. Giant leather couches and chairs were sprinkled generously around, and modern lamps blossomed at intervals. There was a gleaming modern kitchen with a built-in dishwasher, an ice-cube machine, and several gadgets that looked like something out of a mad scientist's laboratory. The bathroom was done in black and white tile. The bedroom was enormous and had a balcony overlooking the mountains and the distant sea.

For a moment she stood looking out at the view, hardly daring to breath for fear all this would vanish and cold reality would descend crashing upon her. This represented success as much as her old apartment represented failure, and there were many times in the past when she'd thought she would never get halfway to where she was now.

"It—it's fabulous," Lois said to Marty, when she could catch her breath.

Marty laughed, pleased. "This is the kind of layout you need to get ahead in this town, kid. It impresses people. You bring a movie producer up here, and he feels like he's a chump if he doesn't give you the lead in his next picture."

He went to turn on the hi-fi set nestled in one corner. "Go check the icebox and see what there is to drink, and I'll put on some celebration music."

Lois found several bottles of French champagne cooling on the top shelf. She brought it out, got some glasses and came back in time to hear a familiar voice cascading into the room from the phonograph.

"Peggy Lee!" she exclaimed.

Marty nodded. "I had an idea she was one of your favorites, kid, so I ordered every Peggy Lee record made. She's worth studying."

They sat together on the couch. Marty opened one of the bottles of champagne and poured drinks for the two of them. Marty raised his glass, touched it to hers.

"To success," he said.

"To success," she repeated.

After several drinks, lulled by the soft music, she began to feel sleepy.

Marty looked at her and wet his lips. "You—you better get out of that dress before you spill anything on it," he said.

Even as he said it, he was busy unzipping her. Lois was beginning to feel drowsy, but she helped shrug off the dress. She felt Marty's hot hands running across her bare shoulders and along the ridge of her bra where it met her breasts. He was having difficulty speaking.

"You'd better go to bed and rest," he said.

She nodded sleepily and didn't resist as he helped her across the living room and into the bedroom. Her shoes dropped off, and she giggled at the soft feel of the carpeting against her naked feet. Marty placed her gently on the bed and then stood for a moment beside her. Just before she closed her eyes, Lois saw him unbuttoning his shirt.

A moment later he was lying on the bed, his body warm against hers, his fingers busying themselves on her bra and panties, and then he was drawing her close. She felt relaxed this time, completely without tension. The champagne had done its work, and she felt much too good to be disturbed by anything he did to her.

This time he seemed more detached and more clinical in his approach. It was almost as if he were testing her for response, studying his effect upon her and wondering if he'd made a good bargain. All this had the effect of making her strive harder to please him, to make sure he wasn't disappointed.

Later, as she lay in his arms, she apologized for being so sleepy.

"That's okay, kid," he said, kissing her. "You've had a pretty full day, and you're not used to the champagne. Living like a human being takes a while to get used to, but you'll be all right. Take it from me, success is gonna fit you like a glove. Right now, just take a nap. Don't bother coming in to the club today. You like your new home?"

She nodded sleepily.

"Good," he said. "I'll give you a call later and maybe we can go shopping for some clothes and things."

"Sure, Marty," she said. She was beginning to drift off again.

"Oh, by the way," he said suddenly, as if it were an afterthought. "I got some other good news for you. I got a call from a friend of mine. Fellow named Jim Fritch, a millionaire oil man from up north. He wants to do a movie down here, and when I mentioned you, he was pretty interested. I know you can fill the bill, but you've got to be nice to him, understand?"

"Uh-huh," she murmured, eyes closed. She smiled to herself. Already Marty was getting her lined up for movie jobs.

"He can do us both a lot of good," Marty said. "But especially you. When he comes down to the club to hear you sing, in maybe a week or two, I want you to be *really* nice to him. Fritch doesn't go for shy girls, and he likes to live it up. Believe me, kid, it's an opportunity any girl would give her eyeteeth for. If he takes a liking to you, you've got yourself a fat part in his movie."

"I'll do my best, Marty," she said, only half listening to his exact words.

"Meanwhile, we'd better start getting your act in shape. You've got a nice voice, but it needs work. First thing tomorrow, you and me and Johnny can get together and go over some of the numbers you've been rehearsing with him."

Lois wanted to go to sleep, but one thought continued to bother her. "Marty," she said, "what about Binnie?"

"What about her?"

"I'm taking her job," Lois said, frowning.

"Don't be silly," he said with a laugh. "Binnie'll be all right. Stop worrying about her, will you? I'll call you later."

Lois mumbled an answer and fell sound asleep.

Marty got up off the bed and gazed admiringly at Lois' nude body sprawled on the sheets. She was a doll, all right, with or without clothes. It was going to be a very profitable relationship.

He dressed and went into the bathroom. Before leaving, he tiptoed into the bedroom to take another look at the sleeping girl. He smiled at the sight of her lying there. Jim Fritch would like her. And so would the others.

All of them.

CHAPTER FIVE

T he Boomerang Club was crowded. Customers huddled around their tables, drinking, talking, listening to the piano in the background. Candles on the tables flickered like fireflies in the darkness.

The audience looked up, suddenly hushed, as a spotlight came on. A girl stepped into the light beside the piano. She was a pretty girl, with a pretty smile, her features framed by a semicircle of casual brown hair, her green eyes glistening almost luminescently. Her firm, youthful figure was encased in a very tight, black-sequined dress, off the shoulder and cut low to show a generous amount of breast and cleavage. She exuded a wholesome sensuality; she was like the girl next door who had developed into a beautiful woman. She nodded in response to the applause that greeted her appearance.

Johnny Kay coaxed an introduction from the keyboard, and Lois leaned back against the piano and sang, softly, certainly, into the microphone. It was still difficult for her to believe that only two weeks ago she had been a waitress out there in the darkness beyond the intimate circle of light, serving drinks, suffering the pain and humility of drunken pinches, wishing she were up there in the spotlight singing. The first night had gone well, but not well enough, and the session had been followed by intense rehearsals—until now, when she was sure of herself and of her audience.

If only her stepmother could see her now.

She felt her skin crawl as she noticed Binnie glaring at her from the bar. For two weeks now, the redhead had been back at the Boomerang working as a waitress and it was obvious that she was displeased at the switch in positions. The glaring still disturbed Lois—not just the glaring itself, but the forceful and constant reminder that Binnie was a living example of how easy it was for a singer in Marty's club to topple off the bandstand and back into a waitress' costume.

Lois shrugged off the unpleasant feelings and directed her attention beyond the brilliant spotlight pinning her against the piano. She felt an almost childish pleasure as she saw Elliot Jordan smiling at her from the near darkness, and she smiled back at him.

It was the third time he had come that week, by himself. Each time, she had hoped he would ask her to have a drink with him, but he hadn't. He had watched and listened carefully, and at the end of each number he had applauded enthusiastically. He seemed to be making notes on a napkin. But nothing else happened.

On the nights she hadn't seen his familiar gray-black head and college-boy smile, Lois felt as though the audience were incomplete.

She was dying to know what he thought of her voice and her technique, but she couldn't go right up to him and ask. He was so important that people were probably always doing it and annoying him, and she didn't want to fit into that classification.

Lois had asked around about him and had seen mentions of him in the trade papers. He had come out to the Coast after producing and directing three of the most successful off-Broadway musical reviews within recent years, and the industry had great hopes for him in television and movies.

She finished her last number and took her bows. Then she deliberately moved in the direction of Elliot's table on her way back to the dressing room. Perhaps he would ask her to sit down. She hoped so. She wanted so much to know what he thought of her—professionally, that is; his comments would be very helpful. But she would have to play the game with care; she could lose him if she threw herself at him. He must have read the write-ups about her in *Variety* and the *Hollywood Reporter*, and the fact that he had come to hear her three times in one week showed that he was interested in her.

She smiled at him as she approached his table, and her heart increased its tempo as she saw him half rise to greet her. She stopped as someone touched her arm.

She turned. "Binnie!"

"You little bitch!" the redhead said coldly.

Lois stared at her, puzzled. "I don't understand."

"You don't, huh?" Binnie said acidly. "Shall I explain it to you out here in front of the world or do we go into your dressing room like ladies?"

"Look, Binnie, could I talk to you later? I've got someone to see and—"

"I'll just bet you have," Binnie said. "Well, he can wait. What I've got to say is more important than you playing footsie with one of Marty's friends."

Lois felt anger boil inside her at the accusation, then she realized it would only harm her to argue out in public. She glanced helplessly at Elliot who was watching her, puzzled, and then she turned and went toward her dressing room. It had been unfortunate timing, but there was nothing she could do about it now.

Once in the dressing room, with the door closed, Binnie carefully scrutinized Lois, walking around and nodding thoughtfully at the hairdo, the dress, the make-up.

"You're living pretty high on the hog these days, aren't you, Lois?" she said coolly.

Lois flushed.

"Yes," Binnie said, still studying her coldly, "pretty high on the hog, I'd say. Not bad for a girl who used to wait on tables just a couple of weeks back. Did Marty get those clothes for you? They don't look like the kind you can buy on waitresses' tips. Not unless you've been serving the customers something besides drinks when you're through here."

Lois glared. "Marty advanced me the money, and I fully intend to pay him back; I even signed contracts to that effect." Then the thought of her explaining it to Binnie annoyed her. "If you want to say something, Binnie, say it. You've obviously been drinking, and I'm too tired to argue with you or try to guess what's on your mind."

"Damn right, I've been drinking," Binnie declared self-righteously. "For two weeks I've been working the tables and getting my bottom pinched, while you're acting like the Queen of Sheba."

"Binnie—"

The smile had faded from Binnie's thin face. "And don't play the sensitive young virgin with me, honey. I've been the route myself. I know what you do in your spare time."

"I don't know what you're talking about. I'm a singer here—and that's all." She ignored Binnie's sarcastic laugh. "Why are you sore at me? Because I got your job? I didn't ask for it. Marty offered it to me. If you've got any beefs, take it up with him."

" 'Marty offered it to me!' " the redhead mimicked. Her face was reddening from anger and from the liquor she'd been consuming. "Where did you hold the audition, his bedroom or yours? Not that I blame him, really. You're a good-looking kid, and you've got the kind of shape Marty and his pals go for. I guess he must be booking you up solid. Who you taking on tonight, honey?"

Lois could feel the anger surging within her, but she clenched her fists in an effort to control it. "Get out of here," she said slowly.

But Binnie was enjoying herself too much to stop. "If Marty ever wants to rig a football game you'd better watch out. You may have to work out with the entire U.C.L.A. football team some night!"

Almost involuntarily Lois' hand shot out at the insult and struck Binnie's cheek with a resounding smack. The blow took the redhead by surprise, and she reeled back, eyes wide, a hand to her stinging cheek.

"You bitch!" Binnie cried. "I'll change that pretty face so not even Dominick will want to look at you!"

"Binnie, I'm sorry. I didn't mean that," Lois said.

"Not as sorry as you're going to be!" Binnie screamed, springing at her.

Lois threw up her hands to ward off Binnie's furious attack. The redhead's nails were long and deadly, and Lois was afraid of the damage they could do to her appearance. A singer couldn't afford to have her face all scratched up. But it was all she could do to defend herself from Binnie's fury.

Desperately, she shoved Binnie aside, threw open the door to the hallway. But the other girl's powerful grip held her. Binnie was screaming vile words and pulling her back into the room. The door slammed shut again.

Triumphantly, Binnie shoved her against the vanity table and tore viciously at her dress.

"Since you're his new star," Binnie shouted, "he can get you another dress. Besides you don't need clothes for what you're doing."

A moment before Lois had been terrified by Binnie's frantic rush, but the redhead's senseless destruction of her costume was more than she could bear. She could partly understand the girl's feelings, but Binnie was like an animal thirsting for vengeance, striking out blindly to maim and destroy.

Anger boiled hotly through Lois' veins as she evaded Binnie's nails, raking at the flesh of her shoulder, and she struck out with a series of hard blows. Surprised, the redhead put her arms around Lois and, in a moment, the two girls fell to the floor, wrestling, kicking, arms flailing, shouting at each other, white thighs flashing in the neon lighting of the dressing room.

Suddenly, Lois felt a strong pair of arms wrench her away from Binnie's iron grip. She looked up to see a tall, husky stranger smiling at her. A second later she saw Marty pinning Binnie's arms behind her back.

"Okay, okay you two, break it up!" Marty was saying.

"You girls play rough," the stranger said, half admiringly, "but I like girls with spirit." He released Lois and handed her his handkerchief. "That pretty face looks like you've been working around an oil rig."

Lois glared at Binnie, then took the handkerchief. It had all been so unnecessary. She could have been with Elliot now, talking to him about her future. Abruptly, she began to sob. She felt the stranger's arms around her, strong, yet gently consoling.

"Get out of here, Binnie," Marty said coldly. "You know I don't allow fights in the club."

"I'm not going anywhere till you explain why you pulled that dirty trick on me," Binnie stormed, "and hired that bitch!"

"Watch your language, lady," the stranger said. "And I'm probably stretching things calling you that."

Binnie turned on him. "And who the hell do you think you are?" she began furiously.

But Marty cut her off. "Binnie, if you don't come with us now, you'll never work for me again. And I'll make sure you don't work anywhere else in this town, either!"

His words had an immediate effect on her. Without another word, she glared at Lois, walked into the hallway and slammed the door behind her.

"I'm sorry, kid," Marty said to Lois. "I didn't think she'd get out of hand that way. You okay?"

Lois nodded, still too shaken to speak.

"This is Jim Fritch," Marty said, indicating the stranger. "You remember I told you about him. Why don't you put on a new face and join us in a while."

"She looks all in," Jim said. "We can make it another night."

Lois looked at him, grateful for his understanding. He was a big man, with black curly hair over a face that was rough-hewn, neither handsome nor ugly but the sort of determined face you'd associate with an oil field. He wore an expensive-looking suit well.

So this was the millionaire oil man Marty wanted her to meet, the one who was going to make a picture and would need a singer.

"I'll send one of the girls back to help you," Marty said at the door. "And don't worry about that dress. We'll get two more tomorrow."

Why not? she thought wearily. *It'll go on my account, along with the Thunderbird and the apartment and everything else, and I'll have to pay you back—one way or another.*

For the first time in two weeks, Lois felt depressed, and the gnawing doubts returned to plague her. She tried to answer Jim Fritch's warm smile, but she felt sick inside. When the door closed behind the two men, she sat silently in front of her vanity table, trying to still the frantic churning of her stomach. She stared unbelievingly at the damage to her dress, hair and make-up. But she knew the damage Binnie wrought went deeper than that, and it wasn't physical.

For the first time, she began to understand how Binnie Jones felt. Marty had simply swept the girl aside, thrown her out like an old pair of trousers that didn't fit him any more. No wonder the girl had been so resentful.

If that was the way these things were handled at the Boomerang, how long would *she* last? Until Marty got tired of her or she put on some weight? Or until some prettier girl came to work at the club?

Her thoughts were interrupted by a soft knock at the door. She looked up to see Johnny Kay's head poking through the open door.

"Hi," he said. "Heard you had some excitement. Okay if I come in?"

"Sure," she said. "Binnie was angry with me for taking her job. I guess I can't really blame for for it."

"Survival of the fittest," Johnny said, closing the door. "It's the code of the West. Or to coin still another phrase, that's show biz."

She couldn't help but smile at him. "You seem happy," she said.

He sighed and slumped down in a nearby chair. "Sheer bravado," he said. He lit a cigarette, inhaling deeply and letting smoke pour from his nostrils. His angular face turned worried. "Unfortunately, I'm about to go to jail."

"What?"

He nodded. "My darling ex-wife wants me to come up with at least a hundred bucks by tomorrow. I'm broke, and payday isn't for another week." He looked up at her. "If I'm in jail I certainly can't earn any money—or help you with the arrangements. I was wondering if maybe—" He hesitated.

"Sure, Johnny, I can let you have it."

"Until payday," he said.

She wrote him a check for a hundred dollars. It made her account a little short, and it was money she'd planned on sending her aunt. But Johnny was a friend in trouble. Besides, she rationalized, she needed him to help her with arrangements.

"Thanks, Lois," he said, leaning to kiss her on the cheek, "you're a doll. I've got to get back to my clamoring public."

He brushed past Marty, who was coming in.

"What did *he* want?" Marty wanted to know.

"He needed some money," Lois said honestly, "for his ex-wife."

Marty grunted his disbelief. "For booze, more likely. You've got to stop worrying about stray cats, kid."

Lois didn't want to argue about it. She wished she'd lied to Marty or been more vague; it wasn't any of his business anyway. She turned her attention to the mirror and saw Marty come up behind her and place his hands on her shoulders.

"What's bugging you, kid? You look as if the earth caved in on you? Is it Binnie? Or is that two-bit piano player bothering you?"

"It's you, Marty," she said slowly. "I've been wondering how long it would be before we repeated that little scene, with me in Binnie's place. How long was Binnie here, six months?"

"You're out of your mind!" Marty barked, his eyebrows coming together in a frown. Then his voice softened. "Look, kid, I *had* to get Binnie out. She was bad for business. Too many people were complaining. She's a nice girl, and I took a chance on her. But L.A. isn't Cincinnati. The competition here is rougher."

"Is that what you'll be telling *me* in six months?"

"Ah, don't be that way, kid. Look, I'm running a night club here, not an amateur show. If it wasn't you, it'd be someone else.

"Now come on. Pull yourself together. You've got a job to do. Play it right with Fritch, kid, and you're in. In six months you won't even consider singing at the Boomerang. Jim was telling me he liked your looks very much, and your voice, too." He hesitated. "It's top secret stuff, and I'm not supposed to tell you, but he told me you look like you'd fit the part, but he has to know you better to make sure. So be nice to the guy and you'll get yourself a nice fat contract as soon as the script rewrites are finished."

All at once, Lois knew what Marty meant by his words "be nice to him." She felt a hard knot in her belly as she remembered his previous words and the whole thing tied up. "Be nice to him, *really* nice." She had been slightly drunk and the words hadn't registered with her. And now there was a new fear in her because she knew how easy it was to be thrown out of the top spot and into oblivion.

Lois nodded, and Marty studied her face in the mirror. He must have sensed the uncertainty in her.

"Now look kid, you want to make good in show business, don't you? Well, act like a pro, for Pete's sake. I'm giving you the chance, so don't muff it. I've got a lot of money tied up in you; that's why I made you sign the notes promising to pay me back."

He went to the door and paused. "I'll expect you at our table in five minutes, okay?"

"Okay," she said, forcing a smile.

Marty was right, and she was beginning to feel like a naïve schoolgirl. Johnny was right, too, when he said it was the survival of the fittest in the Hollywood jungle. She had to be a pro if she wanted to be one of the survivors, and it would be stupid if she muffed her chance just because she had to pay for a chance to make the big time. *You're not a high school virgin any more,* she told herself.

A moment later she was in the darkened club, threading her way among the candlelit tables to where Marty and Jim Fritch were waiting for her. Both men rose in greeting, and the oil man's eyes gleamed with sincere admiration.

"I was just telling Marty how much I enjoyed your singing," Jim said. "And your looks, too. With a combination like that you should go far in show business."

"Thank you," Lois said.

"Say, I've got an idea," Jim said. "What do you say we do a little high-class pub crawling. I get restless sitting too long in one place. How about it, Marty, want to see what the competition is doing?"

Marty smiled and shook his head. "I've got things to do here, but you two run along and have fun. I'll buzz you tomorrow, Jim. Take good care of my star performer here."

"I'll do that," Jim said. "We'll hit every spot on the strip."

I'd like to have a thousand bucks for every spot we don't hit, Lois thought as she got up. *I could pay off Marty the money I owe him!*

She had no doubt that they would wind up in Fritch's hotel suite after two or, at most, three stops. Fine. She was through with that naïve bit, finally. If it was part of the deal—and it always seemed to be—she would have to go along with it. What bothered her was whether she would panic when he tried to make love to her. She had been able to do it with Marty, but it had been easier because she worked at the club and had gotten to know him. This time a perfect stranger was going to ask her to sleep with him on their first date.

Why not? she asked herself. The job Marty had in his pocket was the reason she had given in to *him.* It would be stupid not to go a little further for an even better job.

As he guided her across the room, she noticed that Elliot Jordan had left his table and was not in sight. They went out front and got into a waiting cab.

"Marty told me you were something special," Jim said as the taxi carried them through the neon-lit Sunset Strip, "but I didn't expect anything like this. If I had, I'd have come down here sooner."

He placed one of his big hands casually on her lap and pressed it a little. "I like the way you sing, Lois. I like the way you look. I like the way you move."

"Marty tells me you'll be backing a picture soon and that you'll need a singer," she said, trying to control her nervousness as his hand pressed the flesh of her thigh.

"That's right," he said, after a moment. "And I'd like you to read for one of the featured roles as soon as we get the final script. I was thinking about that while you were singing. I want a gal who can sing and who has a nice body." He ran a finger exploringly down from her knee. "You fit both categories."

"Thank you," she said.

His touch was beginning to make her nervous, and she tried not to squirm away from his hand. It was to her benefit to be nice to him, and she wanted to desperately. But she was not used to being manhandled in the back of a taxi like this. She fought down an impulse to move away, and merely put a restraining hand on his fingers as they began to inch along under the hem of her skirt. Her gesture puzzled him at first, then he smiled and took the hand away from her leg.

"You don't like it in a taxi, eh?" he said sympathetically. "Don't blame you. Hell of a place to do anything. I know girls hate it. Makes them hot and messy."

He contented himself with an occasional squeeze of her thigh, his eyes staring hungrily at her full breasts exposed by the low-cut dress. She sighed inwardly with relief. She didn't know what she might have done if he had put his hand up her skirt. She didn't want to offend him, but calmly accepting sexual maulings from a stranger was not easy. She had barely controlled an urge to rake his hand with her nails. Which would have tossed her chance at a featured role in his movie right down the drain. Still, one thing she could not take was being manhandled as if she were some slut or one of Marty's call girls. It made her angry just to think of it.

They went to the Crescendo, but she barely listened as Mort Sahl went through his act. She was too conscious of Fritch's leg against hers, too frightened that he would reach under the table and squeeze her leg in public. To steady herself, she drank more champagne than she would have ordinarily. She had eaten lightly, as she always did before going on at the Boomerang, and the champagne affected her very quickly.

After several drinks she felt much more relaxed, and when they left the club and got into the taxi again, she didn't resist when Fritch leaned over to kiss her full on the lips. His hand reached into the opening of her dress and cupped her breast over the bra and squeezed, and only then did the knot of worry return. She wondered if the cabbie was looking in the mirror and leering at her.

At Frascati's the tinkle of the piano was drowned out by a tidal wave of thoughts concerning what would come next. The more Fritch drank, the rougher he seemed to get, and the bolder. This time he rested his hand on her leg, under the table, and kneaded the flesh there. If the pattern kept on, by the fourth club, he would rape her right in front of everyone.

"I—I think we'd better leave," she said.

"Sure," he said agreeably, "anything you say, Lois."

Once they were on their way he seemed to forget what he had said about making love in a taxi. She cringed and peeled his grasping fingers from her flesh. She wanted to shout at him to leave her alone, that she wanted to go home—but she kept silent and thought about the movie job he had to offer.

He told the cabbie to take them to the Beverly Hilton, and she knew the moment of reckoning had arrived. She wanted that movie job, she wanted it badly, and she'd get it no matter what she had to do. But it was an intellectual response to the situation. Her emotional reaction was another thing. She thought of what might happen if he tried to rip her clothes off or tried to hurt her. She'd heard stories from some of the girls at the Boomerang about drunks and the things they did when they were alone with a girl. Some of them turned mean and began to tear at your dress and underclothes and even at your body. Others turned raucously insulting and took a sadistic pleasure in making you feel like a common streetwalker.

Fritch had been drinking heavily, and was now getting rougher and cruder. She could control her strong distaste for going to bed with him because the job was so important—but suppose he wanted more than that. Her fear of what might happen was so real it was like a dry rag in her mouth as the cab drew up to the hotel.

"Jim," she said nervously, "I—I'm very tired, really, and I'm sure you must be. Would you mind if I went right on home? I've had a wonderful time, but I am pretty beat and—"

He stared at her, unbelieving. "You want to go home?" he asked. "You're kidding. Listen, I've got something that'll make you feel great in two minutes. I drink it as an eye opener myself every time I go on a pub crawl."

When she hesitated, he seemed to sober up. The driver looked back at them questioningly.

"It's up to you, Lois," Jim said quietly. "The driver can't park here too long. He'll take you home if you really want to go. But I hope you're not serious."

She hesitated, not knowing which way to jump, what to say. She realized it had been a vain hope to think there might not have been any discussion about her decision.

"Jim" she said, placing a hand gently on his arm, "I hope you understand. I'm—well, I'm just played out."

"Sure," Jim said, with exaggerated politeness. "I understand. Well, it's been nice, Lois. Really nice." To the driver he said, "Take the lady home, or anyplace she wants to go."

He took a bill from his pocket and held it out to the cabbie. Something in his voice, a hint of resignation, of mentally turning his back on her, made her shiver with the realization of what she had done. She felt as though something she wanted very badly was slipping between her fingers merely because she didn't have sense enough to close her hand. As he started to leave, she took hold of his sleeve.

"Could a girl change her mind?" she asked. "I guess I'm too keyed up to go to sleep just yet anyway. I'd like to try that eye opener of yours."

He turned toward her with a broad smile. "That's the girl," he said approvingly to her. And to the cabbie he added, "Looks like you've lost a couple of customers, friend."

Lois frowned at the knowing grin on the cab driver's face. *The hell with him,* she thought belligerently as she got out of the taxi, *and the hell with everyone else, too.* She was doing it because she had to do it, and that was the only reason.

Jim Fritch's suite on an upper floor of the swank Beverly Hills Hotel was the most luxurious Lois had ever seen. It rivaled Marty's furnishings and did not have to suffer the curse of heliotrope. While she admired the view of the glittering city from the veranda, Jim was busy on the phone.

"Send up two bottles of French champagne," he said. "Mumms or Moet and Chandon, if you've got it, and some Guinness Stout. Iced. Oh, and a tray of cold cuts." He turned to Lois and asked, "You like caviar and goose liver pâté?" When she nodded, he added them to the list.

Then he switched on an expensive-looking console radio and smiled at her. He was still obviously under the influence of the large quantities of alcohol he'd consumed, but under more familiar surroundings he seemed to contain it better. In fact, he seemed suddenly to have adopted the air of a small boy who was pleased with himself and was trying to impress her.

The thought was so amusing and somehow out of place that she couldn't help but smile. The smile made her feel better and less tense, and she sat in one of the comfortable armchairs and regarded him quizzically. She still felt light-headed, and in the indirect lighting of the room Jim didn't seem nearly as formidable as he had in the close quarters of the taxi.

"I didn't know you were the cavier type," she said.

"I'm crazy about it," Jim said, grinning and flopping himself down in a nearby chair. "I look like what I am—an Okie from a whistle stop near Tulsa you never heard of—but believe it or not, I've been all over this earth, and when I find something I like anywhere I stock up. Back in Bakersfield I've got enough of the genuine caviar stashed away to feed an army. I don't know if you noticed I asked for Persian caviar. I first ate the stuff two years ago when I flew over to Teheran to negotiate a big oil deal and my opposite number threw us a big party. I fell in love with it then.

"Same thing with pâté. I had that at Maxim's in Paris. Up to then I'd always asked myself why the hell they made such a big fuss over liver paste. But the stuff's different, they fill it with truffles—a kind of nutty thing they dig up in the ground with the help of pigs."

Lois found herself more at ease with him. His obvious pleasure in everything he did was so infectious she began to laugh. He was childishly proud of having met six kings and ten prime ministers during his travels, of prowling through the streets of Dahran in Arabia, Caracas and Hong Kong. He told her about himself with such boyish candor that she felt older than he was. When the wine came, he took great care to mix the champagne and Guinness in the proper proportions, using a giant goblet as a mixing bowl.

"I picked this up at the Ritz in Paris a year ago. I was on some toot or other and beginning to poop out around one a.m. Well, this diplomatic guy I'm with tells me he'll fix me up with a special medicine—and this was it. I thought he was nuts mixing English beer and French wine. Now, I swear by it. Go ahead and have some. I make the best Black Velvet you ever drank, lady."

Lois tried a sip, followed it by another, and decided it was a wonderful combination. In a few minutes they were drinking quantities of it and eating the caviar and pâté. The Black Velvet, the food, the lilting music from the radio made her feel as though she were on some voyage far from land. Whatever nervousness she had felt about coming upstairs with Jim had been lulled completely.

"I—I'm sorry about what happened in the taxi," he said. "I guess I was just trying too hard. You're not like the others, I should have known that from the start."

She didn't resist as he stood beside her, took her hands in his and pulled her up beside him. He kissed her and his large hands moved over her body, tentatively at first, and she felt herself shuddering, frightened that he would be rough. Her breath caught as he put his hand over her breasts and then into the neckline of her dress. But his hands were gentle, as though he had learned how she liked to be treated. Even so, she could not control her palpitations or the perspiration that dampened her forehead.

"Don't be afraid, honey, I'm not going to hurt you," he said softly as he felt her shiver against him. "Don't be scared."

He took her arm and led her across the room and into the bedroom. He pressed her down on the bed and then lay beside her. She could smell the cologne he used as he pressed his cheek against hers. The alcohol she'd consumed was taking effect, and she felt her tenseness fading even as his hands moved across her breasts and over her stomach and legs. The pressure of his big fingers kneading the taut flesh of her thighs made her wonder about him.

He seemed to possess a gentleness and a patience alien to his actions in the taxi. It was as though he had fathomed her difficulty and didn't want to rush her, and she felt grateful for his understanding. They lay there for perhaps twenty minutes, not talking, just getting used to each other's presence, while his hands made restless forays under her dress.

"You're beautifully built, honey," he said after a while. "I thought Marty was exaggerating when he told me about you. But you've got it where it counts. Now, let's take this nice dress off before it gets mussed up."

With a finesse that probably came from much practice, he slipped her dress from her, and then the slip. Then he propped himself up on one elbow and studied her as she lay back on the bed clad in her black silk panties and brassiere. He whistled softly and shook his head.

"Marty must want that oil stock pretty bad," he said. "If I had anything like you around, I'd keep it to myself."

For a long moment, he seemed satisfied merely to look at her, his eyes fascinated by her hard, firm breasts, her long tapering legs in their black nylon stockings, the whiteness of her skin against the flimsy black undergarments.

He seemed warm, tender and very human, but she still couldn't help remembering that she was doing this to get a part in a movie. As with Marty, she tried her best to relax completely, only to find that there was something in her which still held her back, at least part way, because it was a cold-blooded business, this using your body to get what you wanted.

Despite this involuntary holding back, she found herself being aroused and responding, to a degree, to his clever and practiced ministrations. She even felt a flicker of irritation because she wasn't hating what was happening to her and cursing the "code of the West" which was forcing her to buy her way to the top.

When Jim had finally worked himself to fever pitch and their coupling was completed, she found herself divided into two people; the one who's body was being used and the one who was able to stand off to one side, watching and disapproving, but still recognizing that this had to be done; the one who made all the appropriate noises and movements, and the one who could be wondering, at the same time, if she would ever sleep with Elliot Jordan.

Now the split in her personality was healed and all of her could concentrate on thinking about sleeping with Elliot Jordan. She hoped it would happen. That frank thought surprised her, and so did the motive behind it. She'd like to sleep with him—not because he could get her into television—because she liked him. It was an absurd thought, and she thrust it from her mind.

She had no idea how many times Jim made love to her. She remembered waking once in his arms and feeling his lips on her breast. She stirred sleepily beneath his caresses, and then fell into a heavy slumber.

It was nearly one o'clock when she awakened to the warm California sun flooding the room. Surprisingly, she felt no hangover and made a mental note to try Black Velvet again. She stretched and yawned the remnants of sleep from her body. As her eyes roamed the large room, she saw a gift-wrapped parcel on the night stand next to her purse. She got out of bed and went to look at it. On top of the package was a sealed envelope with her name written on it in a firm, masculine scrawl. She opened it curiously and read the note inside:

> Dear Louis: I had an early appointment so I left around 8:30. On the way back I picked up a little something for you and dropped it off. Hope it fits. If not, they'll exchange it. Did I remember your measurements okay? I should. How could I forget? I'll be away most of the day, but I'll be back around five-thirty. I put an extra key in your purse so you can leave if you have to. But how about dinner later?
>
> Jim

She tore the fancy wrapper off the box and opened the tissue inside. The box held one of the loveliest nightgowns she had ever seen, made of the sheerest black material trimmed with gold. It was from the most expensive women's shop in Beverly Hills, a place she had passed many times, stopping only to press her nose hungrily against the window to admire some of the merchandise displayed there. Their cheapest item was sold at what to her was an astronomical price, and she had never dared even go in.

With a squeal of delight, she slipped the nightgown over her shoulders, delighting in the expensive rustle of it against her naked body. She stood in front of the mirror and posed, moving first one way and then another to see herself and how she looked.

It was beautiful, and it fit her perfectly, showing off seductive glimpses of her body through the material.

Looking back on the night before, she decided it hadn't been so bad, after all. He was a nice guy and he wanted to see her again, and there was that part in the picture to look forward to. When she picked up the envelope again, she discovered something else that was enclosed there, another piece of paper that she withdrew and held in her hands uncertainly.

Her first feeling was one of deep chagrin. The portrait of Benjamin Franklin on the one-hundred-dollar bill seemed to stare at her with a bland contempt. And then she felt hot anger surge through her, and she crumpled the money into a tight little ball and threw it on the floor.

The bastard, she thought. *The dirty, no-good bastard! Giving me a hundred dollars for sleeping with him—as though I was some damned call girl who did it for money!*

On the heels of that came another thought, one that made her close her eyes and clench her fists in an effort to keep the thought from blossoming full-blown in her mind. But it blossomed all the same, and she felt sick and ashamed with the realization.

Perhaps she'd been fooling herself, and Marty and his chums and even the other girls at the club who were talking about her all knew the truth. Maybe she *was* a call girl!

CHAPTER SIX

"Masters speaking," Marty's business voice came over the phone.

"Marty, this is Lois."

"Oh, hi, kid. Everything okay?" he asked affably.

"No, everything is not okay!" she said irritably. "I have no intention of becoming one of your call girls!"

"So who's asking you to?" he wanted to know, his voice calm and unruffled.

"Well ... your friend Fritch left a hundred-dollar bill for me. What the devil did you tell him, anyway? I hope you made it clear that I'm a singer, not a hustler."

"Hey, take it easy," Marty said, laughing. "Are you at your place?"

"Yes," she said. "I took a cab."

"And the hundred, I hope."

Lois felt the blood mount her cheeks. "Yes," she said after a moment's hesitation. "I—I didn't have any money for the cab so—"

"Look, there's no need to fly off the handle. Come on over for lunch and we'll talk about it."

"I don't think there's anything to discuss," she said sulkily.

"Come on, kid, you've got it all wrong. Come over and have a bite. Ramon is making a Filipino dish with pineapple."

"But—"

"No buts," he said crisply. "You want to talk, we'll talk. I'll tell Ramon to set another place."

Before she could protest, he hung up. She stared at the dead phone, thinking she should call him back. Except maybe it was just as well she saw Marty and set him straight. Sleeping with a guy to get a job you wanted was one thing; being paid for doing it was another. Marty had to understand that.

She went to take a shower. Then she was trying to select a dress when the phone rang. She stamped over to it. If it was Jim Fritch—

"Hello," she said into it harshly.

"This is Elliot Jordan," a male voice said. "Did I interrupt something?"

"No, no," she said, surprised at the elation that flowed through her suddenly. "I thought it was somebody else—somebody I don't like."

"Well, I hope I don't fit into that category. I was going to ask you to have a drink with me last night, and you veered off before I could assure you that leprosy isn't really contagious."

She laughed. "It didn't have anything to do with you, Mr. Jordan—"

"Elliot," he insisted. "And I'll call you Lois."

"Elliot," she said. "I—I had an important discussion with the former singer at the club."

"Binnie Jones?" he said. "I remember her. She wasn't too good." He was silent for a moment, and then he said quietly, "I'd still like to meet you. Have you had lunch yet?"

It was her turn to be silent. The surprise of his calling was still with her, and now it was followed by the surprise of his asking her out for lunch.

He added quickly, "I'd like to tell you a few things about your act, things I've noticed that—" He paused again, then rushed, "Oh hell, that's not true. I do have some suggestions for you, but that's an excuse, not a reason. I'd just like to meet you, that's all. If you've got a policy of not mixing with your fans—"

"No," she said hastily. "Can you hang on while I light a cigarette?"

She put the phone down and stared at it uncertainly. It was a break she'd been hoping for. Elliot Jordan was a rising wheel in the TV industry. What's more he seemed like a nice guy. But Marty was expecting her, and he'd be angry if she stood him up.

She picked up the phone and said, "I'll be happy to have lunch with you—Elliot."

"Wonderful!" he said in an obviously pleased voice. "I'll pick you up. Where do you live?"

She gave him the address.

"In fifteen minutes?" he said.

"Make it a half-hour. I've got to put on a new face."

"It couldn't be nearly as good as the old one," Elliot said. "By the way, do you like Chinese food? I'm a nut on it myself, but I do eat other things. We can have French, Italian, anything you say."

"No, I like Chinese food," she said.

"Good, I'll make us a couple of reservations."

It was a minute after he'd hung up before she could convince herself that he'd really called. Elliot Jordan was picking her up, taking her out to lunch. Even Marty couldn't complain about that, although she should probably call and tell him what he could do with his Filipino dish, complete with pineapple. The hell with him! It would do him good to wait for her. It might show him she wasn't someone he could move around like a chess piece with no regard for her feelings.

Returning to her bedroom, she selected a dress she liked personally and thought Elliot might approve of—a simple black one without ornamentation. She was applying the final touches of make-up when the doorbell sounded.

"Hi," Elliot Jordan said as she opened the door for him.

"Hi," Lois said back at him.

It was the first time she'd seen him in the daytime, and she was pleased that he didn't need the dimness of a night club to look intriguing to her. He was dressed in a white sport shirt, cool gray slacks and a dark blue blazer that made him look like a college boy. His eyes were grayish-blue, she noticed, and very steady as he looked at her.

"The new face looks exactly like the old one," he said, nodding approval. "Which just proves you can't improve on perfection."

She laughed delightedly at the compliment. Her reading had told her he was about thirty-four years old, and only the hints of gray through his closely cropped dark hair made her assign that many years to him. From a distance, he could have been anything from twenty-five to thirty.

"You're sort of cute yourself," she said, on impulse.

The impulse surprised her, since it was really the first time she'd met the man. But she didn't feel nervous or in awe of him, even though he was important to her. It was as though he'd come calling for her many times before, and would again.

"Ruggedly handsome is what the fan clubs would say," he told her.

"You have a fan club?"

He pretended surprise. "Of course. Doesn't everybody?"

"I don't."

"Of course you do. I started one the first time I saw you, even before you became a singer."

Lois had to laugh at the way he said it. She was becoming more and more aware of him as a person, and more than that, as a person she liked—and not just as a man who could do her career some good. She liked his infectious smile, the way he made her feel important, interesting.

He leaned forward and kissed her lightly on the forehead, then took her arm and guided her into the living room.

Lois was startled by the maneuver. His lips had merely brushed her skin but the memory of them still seemed to burn delightfully on her forehead. It had been an innocent, casual gesture, and wasn't really a pass in the normal sense of the word. Elliot was unlike any man she'd ever known, and Lois wondered what new adventures lay before her.

He led her onto the street, where his black Alfa Romeo sports convertible waited at the curb, the top down. He held open the door for her, then got in on his own side and drove off.

As they accelerated through the afternoon traffic, Lois glanced at his profile. It was a good-looking, honest face. She wondered why he'd never been married; some of the accounts she'd read had listed him as one of the most eligible bachelors in the entertainment industry. He glanced over at her and smiled, and Lois knew that Elliot had no idea she was anything more than a night club singer; his look at her had told her that, and she was glad. She wondered if he would look at her in the same way if he knew. Hastily, she thrust that thought from her mind. She was acting like a high-school girl with a crush on a football hero. A date for lunch did not mean a romance. What did it matter what Elliot thought? Yet she knew that it did matter. It seemed like such a long time since a man had been interested in her for herself and not her body.

"A nickel for your thoughts," he said, and when she looked over at him in surprise, he added, "Prices have gone up."

She laughed. "I was just thinking how well you drive," she said.

"I used to race," he said. "I thought I'd do some more when I got out here on the West Coast, but so far I haven't had time. It's come in handy, though, for your freeways."

They arrived at Wong How's on Pico Boulevard, and he skillfully maneuvered the small car into a parking place. He got out, held the door open for her, and they went into the restaurant. It was crowded, but the headwaiter greeted Elliot by name and led them past booths and tables to a corner booth with a reserved sign, which he removed as they seated themselves.

Lois busied herself studying a menu the size of an election poster. After a while, Elliot said, "If you've never had it, I'd suggest the—" and he said something that sounded almost unpronounceable.

"The what?"

Elliot laughed. "I've got an idea. Why don't you have faith in my judgment and let me do the ordering."

"All right," Lois said.

She wasn't the least surprised that she *did* have faith in him. She had a feeling he would know instinctively what she would like. There was just something about him that inspired such confidence, not merely his clean, fresh appearance, but his attitude, his directness, his apparent honesty.

She listened, enraptured, as he consulted the menu and ordered things she had never heard of, using their Chinese names, pronouncing the words confidently to the waiter.

"Where did you pick all that up?" she asked, astonished, aware of the admiration in her voice.

He grinned and shrugged. "I was one of those characters the Army sent to Harvard during the war to learn Chinese. Eight hours a day, five days a week, and you have to absorb a few things, even if it's by osmosis."

The disclosure about himself triggered a series of reminiscences about his service in Korea, his trip to Europe, his work in New York. He had drifted into the theater after the war had interrupted his studies at law school. He'd always been interested in theater, so in the service he set about organizing soldier shows.

"Irving Feinman, the Broadway producer, caught one of them," he said, "and I got an invitation to become his man Friday. Greatest piece of luck anyone ever had in his life. Contacts are very important in this business."

"You had more than contacts," she said. "You'd have to be pretty good to get the job you have out here."

He laughed good-naturedly. "You've been reading my publicity blurbs. Oh, I know I have some talent. But it doesn't mean a damned thing unless you can get someone to open a few doors for you. I'd probably be a lawyer now if Feinman hadn't seen my army show. That contact led to everything else.

"But I needn't be telling you all this," he went on. "You probably had to knock on a thousand doors yourself, and apparently you found the right one. You were a waitress just a couple of weeks ago."

"Yes," she said.

She felt the color rising to her cheeks. Again she wondered if he knew about her; it was unnerving not knowing. Fortunately, the food arrived, and she was grateful for the interruption. Some of the food was recognizable—like the soup and the spareribs and the shrimp—but even that had been exposed to some culinary magic that delighted her taste buds.

She thought about Marty and Jim Fritch, and of what Elliot had said concerning the opening of doors. Even Elliot knew that talent was not enough, but would he approve of the way she was getting her doors open?

During the meal he talked about his experiences, his plans for the future, the projects he was currently working on—not in an effort to impress her, but as one friend to another. She listened, fascinated, sipping from the ceramic teacup. It was a shock when she looked up to see the ornate hands of a wall clock pointing to three o'clock.

Marty! she thought. *He's still waiting for me.*

"Something wrong?" Elliot asked, seeing her face.

"I was supposed to meet someone," she said.

He glanced at his watch. "I'm sorry. I didn't realize it was so late. We'd better go."

They drove to her apartment, and as they parked in front he took her hand and held it for a moment.

"I've enjoyed being with you, Lois," he said sincerely. "I hope we can do it again sometime soon."

"I'd like that," she said, then hesitated. "Elliot," she said finally, "I—I do like you, very much, but I can't help but wonder how you happened to pick me. There are lots of girls in this town who would give their right arm to go out with you, girls who are prettier, more talented—"

He laughed. "First of all, I am not collecting girls' right arms. Second of all, I didn't pick you; you were picked out for me."

She felt cold. *By Marty?* she wondered. "By whom?"

"Nobody. No person, anyway." He shrugged. "Call it Fate, if you like, though that's a little corny. It's actually probably much simpler, something like a chemical reaction that happens when a boy and a girl meet. It happens all the time— but not to me, so when it does I pay attention. Any more questions?"

She shook her head happily. "Not right now."

"I lead a kind of crazy life, with rehearsals at all hours. But I would like to see you again. There's a sports-car race coming up at Santa Barbara; maybe we can sneak up there for an afternoon. Anyway, I'll call you and drop in at the club to hear you sing once in a while."

He leaned over and kissed her lingeringly on the cheek, hesitated briefly, and then brushed his lips against hers. Lois could feel her blood race in response. Then he straightened, got out and helped her from the car. A moment later, he waved to her as the small black Italian car roared away from the curb.

Remembering Marty, she hurried. Not bothering to change her dress, she went right out to the carport, got into the Thunderbird and drove off. He was furious when she finally got there at 3:30.

"What the hell do you mean standing me up over two hours?" he shouted at her. "After I tell Ramon to knock himself out making his specialty. The guy's ready to quit on me."

"I'm sorry," she said. She'd decided not to tell him about Elliot. "I lay down for a nap, and I guess I overslept."

"Don't lie to me!" Marty snapped. "I've been calling you all afternoon. You'd have heard the phone beside your bed unless you were stone deaf."

"Okay, okay," she almost shouted back at him. "I was sore. I was good and sore because you set me up as a call girl—when I specifically told you I wouldn't play that way."

Marty's eyes narrowed warily. "Who said you were a call girl? You were just being nice to a guy who can give you a big job, that's all."

"What about this?" she said, annoyed, pulling a wad of bills from her purse. "I got a hundred dollars and a seventy-dollar nightie this morning. What do you call that? "

Marty grinned. "What're you getting so riled up for, kid? Okay, so big Jim gave you a gift and sweetened it with a C-note. Why should you complain about that? He's that kind of a guy. Money doesn't mean anything to him. He sprinkles it around like water. I'll bet he gave the cabbie triple the fair and the doorman enough to buy him two meals. You should see what he gives the girls at the club just for bringing him a drink."

"A hundred dollars is a lot of money," Lois insisted. "He was paying me off and I don't like it. That's not why I went to bed with him and you know it."

"Sure, kid, I know it and you know it and Jim knows it, too. You've got it all wrong. The C-note was a gift, just like the nightie. When Jim wants to do something nice for somebody who makes him feel good, he sometimes gets carried away with generosity. He gives gifts, money—parts in pictures." He shrugged. "You can send the money back to him if you want to, but then he'd be sore and you'd just spoil everything. Right now, he thinks you're terrific."

"Oh? How do you know?"

"He called me about an hour ago. He raved about you, said you were everything I'd told him, and that he was telling his director to give you an audition as soon as the script rewrites are finished."

Her anger faded before his words. "An audition?"

Marty nodded. "He assured me you'll get first crack at the role no matter who they asked already. That means a screen test and the works."

Lois' eyes widened. "Did he really say that? That I'll get a screen test for the part?"

"His exact words," Marty said. "You should have heard him on the phone."

She sat down to catch her breath. "My God, that's—that's wonderful."

"I told you," Marty said. "Now, let's have a drink to celebrate." He poured two drinks from a decanter on a side table and said: "But we don't just sit still waiting. This role is one of the featured parts, the second lead. Meanwhile, I want to get you known around town as a performer, maybe get you some TV work."

"Oh, that would be wonderful, Marty. Can you arrange that?"

"I think so—if you'll play along like a trooper and stop acting like a kid out of school."

Her face fell and she felt cold again. "You mean more Jim Fritches." It was a statement, not a question.

"What the hell's the matter with you, Lois?" he asked impatiently. "Of course, I mean more Jim Fritches. You think one contact is going to last you a lifetime? I know a couple of guys who can get you all kinds of short cuts. Or would you prefer sitting in agents' anterooms? Look, kid, you haven't been singing here long enough to get you known, and let's face it, you need these guys a helluva lot more than they need you. If all they wanted was a roll in the hay, they could have any girl in town. Sure they do me favors, but they expect a certain amount of gratitude in return. Don't blame me for the facts of life in this business, for Pete's sake. I didn't make the rules."

Lois was silent for a long while. She was remembering that there were at least a thousand girls for every job in Hollywood and it wasn't necessarily the girl with the most talent who got the job. And she recalled what Elliot had said about all the talent in the world not doing you any good if you couldn't be seen.

"All right, Marty," she said, resignedly. "Do what you have to. But just don't palm me off to anyone as a call girl." She looked up at him, her green eyes alive with determination. "I mean it, Marty."

"Sure, kid, don't worry about it," he said, patting her on the arm. "Everything'll work out fine."

"Especially for you," Lois said drily. "I helped clinch your little oil deal for you, didn't I? Jim told me about it."

"Why not?" Marty said agreeably. "The more I do for you, the greater your chances of paying me off and moving on to bigger and better things. You don't think I'm helping you just because I'm a boy scout?"

"No," she admitted, "I certainly never thought that."

He ignored the tinge of sarcasm in her voice. "But you'll profit by all this, kid, and don't forget it. That role will move you up a couple of light years in show business. Just think of how good your picture will look in the Academy Catalogue the casting directors use here. Your photo and a major film credit next to it. You'll have agents all over town trying to sign you up. Maybe I can help you there, too; I know some of the biggest flesh peddlers in Hollywood—" He caught the look on her face and added quickly, "I—uh—shouldn't have used that expression. Say, how would you like to meet Tony Formio?"

"The one with National Artists?" she said surprised. "You know him?"

Marty grinned expansively. "I know everybody. Tony and I belong to the same athletic club. And we've worked together on a few business deals."

"That would be marvelous," Lois said, feeling an excitement beginning to flow through her again. "I think I've tried to see somebody at National Artists at least half a dozen times and just got the runaround. My God, when I think of what that could mean—"

"A lot," Marty said. "They not only represent talent, they create their own package deals in pictures, TV, night club acts, everything."

"Oh, Marty, if you only could," she said.

His words had rekindled her dreams of hitting the big time. Getting in with a top agent meant doors opening for you everywhere.

"No trouble, kid, as long as you co-operate. I'll give Tony a call and have him get in touch with you."

Lois hesitated, then said, "Can't the three of us just get together, maybe for dinner, and talk it over?"

"You're starting to go back to that dream world again," he said, irritation putting an edge to his voice. He sighed impatiently. "Look, kid, either you take my advice and do as I say—or let's forget the whole thing."

"No," she said quickly. "I just don't want to see a lot of men, Marty. I don't want a reputation for that."

"I understand. Anybody I send you will be a valuable contact. I guarantee it," he said solemnly.

"All right, Marty," she said wearily. She felt tired, as though she'd just fought a battle and lost it. "I guess I'll go home and rehearse a few numbers."

Marty looked her up and down and wet his lips. He opened his mouth as though he were going to ask her something, then changed his mind.

"Sure, kid. Go home and relax." He walked with her to the door and then he said, "Oh, by the way, I'd better warn you about Tony Formio."

"Warn me about what?"

"Well, he's something of a pill. A real cold fish. Lots of big men in this town are a little screwy in some department or other. Well, that's Tony's problem."

"He won't try to hurt me?" she said worriedly.

"No, no, nothing like that. But he can get a little unpleasant." He paused and watched her face. "Of course, if you want to skip him—"

"No," she said quickly. "I'll see him."

He put his arms around her and kissed her lightly.

"That's my girl. Go home now and rest. You got a big evening ahead of you."

CHAPTER SEVEN

Four days later the phone rang about two o'clock in the afternoon, and when Lois answered it a cold voice said, "This is Tony Formio. Lois?"

"Yes, Mr. Formio," she said nervously.

"You busy about four this afternoon?"

"No."

"I'll be over."

He hung up.

Lois stared at the phone in her hand, slightly bewildered by the abruptness of the call. Then she shrugged and replaced the phone in its cradle. Marty was right. Formio was a cold fish, all right. His tone had been matter-of-fact, businesslike.

But, she reminded herself, cold fish or not, he was still Tony Formio. With his partner, Harry Ponce, he ran one of the biggest talent agencies in the world. Though not as big as MCA or William Morris, it represented some of the biggest names in Hollywood, television and on Broadway, names that were almost household words throughout the country. His name or his partner's name appeared in the trade papers at least two or three times a week. They were involved in all kinds of big-name package deals. If a multimillion-dollar picture was announced, there was a good chance that National Talent supplied the stars and the director, and sometimes even put up some of the money. They supplied big time acts to the Copa in New York, the Pump Room in Chicago, and the various night-club palaces in Las Vegas. They helped put together television series, spectaculars, everything.

Both Formio and Ponce had reputations for being shrewd and ruthless negotiators. They also had reputations for being completely uninterested in their clients unless they were big money-makers and could be used as pawns in summit-level show business deals. As a result, they were disliked by many producers, actors, writers and directors. But the same people were likely to accept a Formio-Ponce client as worth his weight in gold where a new film or TV show was concerned.

Whether he was a cold fish or not, Tony Formio was important to her. If he liked her and signed her up as a client and then tried to find her a spot in a first class cabaret or a film, she was really on her way.

She went into the bathroom, drew a tubful of water, added bubble bath, and relaxed in the warm water. The phone rang once while she was there, but she knew she'd never get to it in time, so she ignored it. It might be Elliot. He'd called her several times during the past four days, just for a chat. Once he picked her up after work and they went out to have breakfast together. He'd invited her to go to Santa Barbara with him the next Saturday for the sports-car races, and she'd accepted with the provision that they get back in time for her stint at the club.

She'd tried to analyze her feelings about Elliot. She was well aware that he liked her, and she knew she liked him, for himself and not because he could help her in her career.

After her bath, she rubbed herself liberally with her most expensive perfume. Then she put on her best afternoon dress, a Jacques Fath model a Beverly Hills coutourier had sold her; the dress favored her hips and bosom, showing them to the best possible advantage. She set out some iced caviar on a side table in the living room, as well as bottles of twelve-year-old Scotch, gin and vodka.

At four-fifteen the doorbell rang and she went to answer it.

"Johnny!" she said, surprised and disappointed.

The lean pianist was obviously drunk. His eyes looked bleary, his long black hair was mussed and he looked like he'd been up all night. In one hand he carried a gaily wrapped package, obviously a bottle.

"Lois, baby," he said.

"Johnny, I can't ask you in now," she said nervously. She looked around him into the empty hallway. "I'm expecting a visitor."

"Oh?" he said, smiling. "Who? Not our great little bossman, I hope. He doesn't like to see me drunk. I *am*. drunk, you know. You may not believe it, 'cause I hold my booze so well, but—"

"Johnny, please!" Lois said, looking anxiously over hs shoulder at the elevator, expecting Tony Formio to pop out of it at any moment.

"Came to see your new place, Lois," he said in a blurred voice, shoving past her into the living room. He hoisted the bottle. "Brought you a little housewarming gift."

She closed the door and followed him. "Please go, Johnny."

He looked hurt. "Bought you the finest champagne on the market. Want you to drink it with me. For old times' sake. Remember old times, Lois when we used to be such great buddies?"

"We still are, but I can't right now. Come over tomorrow."

He shrugged, looked disappointed, then headed toward the door. He stopped suddenly.

"Can you let me have a couple of bucks?"

"But I gave you a hundred dollars yesterday," she said, astonished. "You told me that was all you needed."

He waved his hands in a helpless gesture. "It was all I needed yesterday. Today I got a wire from my ex-wife in San Francisco. Says I'm way behind in child support and she'll get the law after me if I don't send her money."

Lois sighed. She had to get Johnny out—fast. "How much do you need?"

"Two hundred," he said, adding quickly, "I'll pay you back as soon as Marty comes through. I swear it."

"If you don't go to the track first, or have to pass a liquor store," she said wearily. "Why do you throw all your money away like that, Johnny? What's the sense of being broke all the time? You told me you wanted to save money so you could take some time off to work on your music."

"I will," he said, "as soon as I get Myra off my back. How can I get any work done when I have her to worry about? Look, if you don't want to give me the money, just say so."

"I didn't say that."

She went into her room and wrote him a check for two hundred dollars. She returned and gave it to him, along with a nudge toward the door.

"Thanks, Lois," he said, "I sure appreciate this. And I promise I'll—"

"That's all right," she said. "Just go before—"

The doorbell rang firmly, cutting off her sentence. Her heart sank as she went to answer it. The last thing she wanted Tony Formio to see was a drunk in her apartment, but there was no helping that now.

In the doorway stood a stout man in an expensive-looking dark suit. He had the coldest eyes Lois had ever seen on a human being, and his mouth seemed to be turned down in a permanent sneer. On his big florid face with its enormous jowls, the man's small mouth looked like a hole drilled into a pumpkin. His head was nearly bald.

"Lois?" he said indifferently.

"Mr. Formio?" she said, forcing a smile. His eyes wrinkled into a frown as he saw Johnny. "Please come in. Mr. Kay was just leaving."

Johnny looked impressed. "Tony Formio of National Talent? Well, this is my lucky day—and yours, too, Mr. Formio." He fumbled in the inside pocket of his jacket and removed a rolled score. "Just happen to have a new song I'd like you to hear—"

"You said you wouldn't be busy," Formio said gruffly, like a judge pronouncing sentence. He turned on his heel and headed for the elevator.

"Please don't go," Lois begged. "Johnny's just going. He dropped by for a moment—unexpectedly."

As Formio hesitated, Lois threw a pleading look at Johnny, who shrugged and put his score back in his pocket.

"Sorry," Johnny said, both to Lois and to Formio, and went down the hallway.

Tony Formio marched into the apartment, settled heavily into the nearest chair, and tapped the end of a fat Egyptian cigarette irritably on a thin gold cigarette case.

"I must have been crazy to listen to Masters," he growled. "All I need is for this to get around town." He jerked his head toward the door. "Who is that lush?"

"Johnny Kay. He works at the Boomerang. He won't say anything."

"All right, all right," he said, cutting her off impatiently. "Look, I haven't got much time." He glanced quickly at a thin gold watch encircling his hairy wrist. "I got all of a half-hour." He favored her with a glacial smile. "Marty tells me you sing."

"Yes," she said hopefully. "I'm sorry you don't have much time. I was hoping you could listen to a few of my numbers. I have some recordings."

"Sure," he said, nodding indifferently. "Some other time maybe. I'll come down and listen to you at the club some night if I have time. I like to help new singers."

"It would mean a great deal to me to be represented by you, Mr. Formio."

"You're right, it would. Well, maybe we can arrange something." He glanced at his watch again. "Well let's get started."

"Can—can I offer you a drink first?" she said uncertainly.

"There's only one thing you can offer me," he said, his cold eyes measuring her figure in a way that made the color rush to her cheeks. "My chauffeur's going to be here in a half-hour.

He put his arm around her waist and moved her firmly toward the bedroom. She was astonished by his manner, but then Marty had warned her. She didn't resist as he led her into the bedroom and closed the door behind them.

He said, "I'll undress you."

She stood still and let him unzip her dress from the back. He did it so roughly she was afraid he'd tear it. She half turned.

"Hold still," he commanded.

She closed her eyes and resisted the impulse to turn around and slug him. "You don't have to bark at me," she said, "I'm not deaf."

"That's my natural tone," he said as he pulled the dress over her head.

He stood back and surveyed her breasts and hips with the thoroughness of an engineer. Without changing his expression, he stepped toward her and cupped one of the breasts, kneading the flesh with the matter-of-factness of a veterinarian.

"Not bad," he said. "I might be able to get you a spot in a road musical. Can you dance?"

"A little," she said nervously.

Tony Formio was rapidly becoming more than a cold fish—he was becoming obnoxious. Lois found herself loathing everything about the man: the heavy touch of his pudgy fingers probing her, unmindful of the diamond ring scraping her skin, his tone of a boss ordering a file clerk around, the way he handled her. But the mention of a job in a big road musical compensated for a lot.

"Sure," he said brusquely. "I'll think about it and call you in a couple of weeks when something opens up."

"Thank you, Mr. Formio," she said gratefully.

"Come here," he said in a flat voice.

She moved toward him, and he removed her brassiere and panties and bent to scrutinize her white thighs and hips.

"You need a tan," he said drily. "Go get a tan. It looks sexy. I like your tits. They're nice. But keep them hard." He flicked imperiously at the nipples. "I can't stand women with droopy tits. I'll let you in on a little secret. Massage them with cocoa butter every week. I got that from one of the top strippers in the country. That's all she's got is big tits. It's her bread and butter, and she has to take care of them. Actually you're better-looking than she is. But watch your figure."

He moved around her and studied her backside. It annoyed Lois to be studied like a shank of beef being examined by a government inspector, but she stood very still, remembering that this man would do her a lot of good.

"Don't get too much on your can either," he said, slapping her buttocks like a man petting a dog. "You're still good there, but keep it that way. I see you even got your Venus dimple."

He traced her Venus dimple right above her buttocks with his forefinger. Her skin crawled and she fought down an impulse to scream. Then, as though he were bored with the whole thing, he took his hand away and began to undo his tie.

"You can lie down now," he said as he removed his jacket. He glanced at his watch and grunted. "Jeez, I hate that damned grind. If I had any sense I'd stay in one town or the other, instead of commuting between Hollywood and New York like a traveling salesman."

Lois crept under the quilt and stared at the ceiling while he undressed and droned on about the S.O.B.'s in the studios who were all thieves, the stupidity of Hollywood directors, the prima donnas among his clientele who used him as a substitute head shrinker.

She tried not to think about him, but it was impossible. He was a big man, and she'd have to remember that. Actually, under other circumstances he might even have been funny, but she had the feeling he would not be funny in bed with her, and as each item of his clothing whispered to the floor she found herself tensing with the dread that was growing in her.

He continued his petulent monotone until he was completely naked and had gotten under the quilt with her. Then, his talking ceased.

He caressed her with neither words nor passion. She felt ill as his pudgy hands moved over her breasts and thighs in a manner befitting the meat buyer of a big hotel inspecting a roast in some market. At least Jim Fritch had shown some tenderness, some acceptance of her as a human being. They had eaten and drunk together, laughed and danced. With Formio it was cold routine. He made love the way he talked: he got it off his chest and then forgot it.

As he embraced her in the act of love, she closed her eyes to shut him out completely from her sight. She thought of Elliot—no, that was sacrilege—she thought of the Boomerang, of people she had known, she recited the multiplication tables. The important thing was to have another image in her mind while he was doing this to her.

Abruptly he finished his minute and clinical problings of her and, without a word, doubled his fist and punched a thigh to signal that he was ready to wind up his would-be love-making.

Lois closed her eyes and feelings to the inevitable and adjusted her position to receive him ...

After a few minutes, he grunted and it was over.

A minute later the phone rang shrilly. It was Formio's chauffeur. When Lois passed the phone to the agent, he said gruffly, "You schmuck. You're always catching me right in the middle. What the hell, have you got X-ray eyes, you bum?" He guffawed loudly and said, "Be downstairs in five minutes. Don't be late, *paisan.*"

"Nice boy," he said to her as he hung up. "He's been my driver for ten years. His Old Man knew my Old Man in Italy."

He rose heavily and went into the bathroom, waddling like an outsized gander. At the door, he turned and said, "Not bad, Lois. Could be better. But you're young yet. Maybe we'll try again."

Not if I can help it, Lois promised silently. She hated Tony Formio, and she hated Marty, and she hated the world for forcing her to do this to make good in show business.

But at least she wasn't doing it just for money, she consoled herself.

Later, when Tony Formio had gone, she discovered two fifty-dollar bills on her dressing table.

CHAPTER EIGHT

Lois was roused from a deep sleep by the shrill ring of the phone beside her bed. After the session with Tony Formio, followed by her stint at the club, she was exhausted. The luminous hands of the clock on the night stand told her it was three-thirty in the morning.

"Lois," an unhappy voice said at the other end. "Lois, baby. Sorry to wake you up."

She tried to blink the sleep from her eyes. "Who is this? Johnny?"

"Yes," he said in a blurred voice. "I'm—I'm in jail."

"In jail? What for?"

"Drunken driving," he said. He rushed on, "Lois, baby, I know I've asked you for a lot of money, but I need help and I haven't anybody else to turn to. I've got a few dollars myself, but I need two hundred fifty more. Can you bail me out, Lois?"

"Two hundred fifty dollars!" she said incredulously. She was fully awake now, shocked out of sleep by his request. "But I gave you two hundred only this afternoon—"

"For my ex-wife," he said. "I sent it to her, and now I'm broke. Honest."

"I've only got thirty dollars left until payday," she said.

"You can get it from Marty," Johnny suggested. "He won't give me any more advances on my pay. I've got to get out, Lois. If I don't show up, Marty'll can me. I won't be able to send my wife money or pay you back. I don't even know if I can get another job."

"Oh, Johnny," she said helplessly, wishing she could find some magic means to straighten him out, "why the devil do you always do this?"

"Don't argue with me now, Lois, please," he begged. "My nerves are shot. I'll explain it to you later. Please go see Marty. If I have to spend another night in this sewer I'll go nuts. It's worse than a pigsty. The place is crowded with pickpockets, drug addicts, homosexuals—"

"I don't know if I can get anything from Marty either," she said. "He's advanced me a lot of money in the last week."

"You've got to try," he said. His voice was plaintive, almost whining, and she found her annoyance with him changing to an overwhelming pity. He was like a stray cat that no one wanted. "You're the only one I can call, the only friend I've got in this lousy town. If I couldn't depend on you, I think I'd end it all."

"All right, Johnny," she said, resignedly. "Tell me where you are."

She wrote down the address of the police station and hung up. It was now three-forty. She knew that sometimes Marty stayed up for a few hours after closing up the Boomerang for the night. Besides, she'd promised Johnny she'd call right away. She dialed the number and breathed a sigh of relief when Marty answered, obviously wide-awake.

"Hello, Marty, this is Lois. Sorry to bother you," she said, "but it's important."

"Feel free to call any time, kid? What can I do for you?"

"I—I need money."

"Oh?"

"Two hundred fifty dollars in cash. I need it right away. It — it's for my aunt in St. Louis."

There was a pause. "I don't know, kid. I've already laid out a potful of dough for you. Can't you give it to her out of your salary?"

"You know I can't," she said irritably. "I get about $150 in take-home pay, and out of that comes money for voice lessons, and—"

He interrupted her with, "Look, Lois, I've already laid out more than I should have. The money for the car, two months' advance on the rent for your aunt. Tell her to wait until payday."

"Marty, I can't. I need it now."

He paused for a moment. "All right, I'll tell you what I can do. I'll give you the money if you'll see a couple of my friends this afternoon."

She reddened and bit her lip. Well, now it was out. There was no doubt about anything now. She was filling Binnie Jones' shoes in every department. Marty Masters' top call girl. She wanted to slam the receiver down on the hook. She wanted to tell Marty to go to hell. Instead, she just sat down on the edge of the bed, slightly stunned.

She thought of Johnny, depressed in the crowded jail cell, depending on her to come to his resuce. There was no doubt that she was his only real friend and that, somehow, she felt responsible for him.

"I can't afford to lay out any more money," she heard Marty's voice saying on the other end of the phone. "Look, kid, this is just a stopgap, that's all. I know a couple of big spenders who are in town on a toot. Between the two of them they'll take care of your financial problem. I'll give you the two-fifty and you can give it back to me after you see these two guys. Okay?"

"Marty," she blurted irritably. "I don't want to be known as one of your pros."

"You're not," he said with an air of offended innocence. "You're doing this because it's an emergency. Believe me, kid, I just can't lay out any more dough right now unless I know I'll get it back tomorrow. It's up to you. I'm not forcing you to do a thing."

"No," she said slowly, "you're not, are you? All right, Marty, I'll be right over."

On the way over to Marty's she tried not to think of what she was going to have to do. She felt sick and ashamed thinking of it, but she couldn't let Johnny down even if he'd gotten himself in the mess. When she was first starting out, Johnny had helped her with arrangements, unselfishly devoted his time and talents to aiding her. If he was fired from his job, he'd have trouble getting another, and it could easily mean the end to his career.

Marty was in his heliotrope pajamas and a bathrobe when he let her in. She hardly glanced at him as she went into the living room.

"Here you are, kid," he said affably, handing her the money. "Two-fifty—just what you asked for. But I was serious about needing it tomorrow. You shouldn't have any trouble getting that out of these two guys."

Lois took the money and put it in her purse without counting it. "Who are they?"

"The guys? Burt Ralston, a big trucking company man who comes to the club, and Si Bender, an accountant I know."

"They're not in show business?"

"They have nothing whatever to do with it," Marty told her honestly. "They're just guys who want a girl. And they want to keep it very private. They've got too much to lose if it got around."

"All right," Lois said resignedly.

Marty laughed and put his arm around her affectionately. "Come on, kid, cheer up. You're a worrier, that's your problem. I can tell you three top stars right now who started the same way. One of them was a call girl in Chicago four years ago, and another starred in stag movies before she ever came out to—" He saw her expression and shrugged. "Okay, okay. I was just trying to explain, that's all."

She turned to go. "Thanks for the money, Marty. I'll give it back to you tomorrow."

He went to the door with her. "What time do you want them over?"

"Any time," she said unenthusiastically. "Have them call me. And Marty?"

He looked at her expectantly, his bland baby face innocent.

I hate you, Marty, for doing this to me, she thought.

"Nothing," she said.

Marty reached out to pat her arm, but she eluded his touch and he shrugged. "You'll feel better tomorrow," he promised.

"Sure," she said.

She was deeply disturbed as she drove down to the jail. The feeling was growing stronger and stronger that she was being caught in a net from which there was no escape. She had no resentment for Johnny because of it. She realized with sudden clarity that it was inevitable that it should come to this. On her salary and with her debt load she would have been forced to play it Marty's way sooner or later, and Johnny's need for help had just advanced the day a little.

That, too, was part of the facts of life in Hollywood. The knowledge did not make the fact any more palatable.

A half-hour later she was handed a receipt for her money and told to wait at the entrance. A moment later, Johnny appeared, looking disheveled and sheepish. Silently, they went out to the pink Thunderbird, got in. As they went down the freeway, Johnny gave her his little boy smile and said, "Thanks a lot, Lois. I really appreciate it, and I'll pay you back, honest."

"Sure, Johnny," she said without looking at him.

"My God, that drunk tank was awful. They're so crowded they're sleeping on the floor in there. And the smell!" He fell silent for a moment, then he said, "Did Marty give you a hard time?"

"No," she said. "He just insisted I see a couple of his pals tomorrow."

It amazed her that she could talk about it so calmly, as though she were talking about someone else who would be seeing a couple of Marty's pals.

"That's his standard procedure with the other kids who need dough. Don't be sore at Marty, Lois, he means well; personally, I think you're smart for wising up. It'll pay all your bills for you, and you'll be that far ahead. It makes a lot more sense than just lugging trays around all day, or even trying to make ends meet by being an underpaid singer at the club."

She didn't say anything. She wanted to tell him to shut up, that she was just going through with this to help him out and that would be it. But once again she wondered if he might not be right. Sleeping with Marty's show business acquaintances didn't seem to be getting her anywhere. Perhaps if she took on a few extra, just for the money involved—

Furiously, she thrust the thought aside.

"Hey, what's the matter?" Johnny wanted to know as the Thunderbird leaped ahead in a swift acceleration.

"Nothing," she said bitterly. "I'm just tired and I want to get home. I've got a busy schedule ahead of me. It looks like I'm about to start out on a long and profitable career—whether I like it or not!"

CHAPTER NINE

I t was a warm Sunday afternoon, and the Santa Monica beach
was crowded when they arrived. Elliot spread the blanket over
an unoccupied area of sand near the ocean, and he and Lois
stripped to their swim sunits.

"C'mon," Elliot said, "let's try that water on for size!"

"You go ahead. I've got to put on my bathing cap. I'll be right
there in a minute."

She put the cap on her head and started tucking her hair
under the rubber edge of it, watching Elliot's trim, athletic figure
sprinting to the foaming surf and into it.

It had been two weeks since Marty's two friends, Burt Ralston
and Si Bender, had both called her for the same afternoon. Marty
was right: neither of the men was interested in any phase of show
business; they wanted one thing, a girl, and they were willing to
pay well for one.

Marty had been persistent in his attempts to get her to see
others, but she couldn't take any more, even with the night club
owner's threats to throw her out on her can. Besides, there was
Elliot and the progress in her relationship with him, and she
knew that she had to stop all evasions and face Marty with her
decision.

Elliot was a startling change from the others. They had managed a Saturday afternoon sports-car race at Santa Barbara, sail-
boating off Catalina Island, several dinners and shows. Not once
had Elliot gone farther than to hold her tightly to him and kiss

her with a tender passion; it seemed as though just being with her was sufficient for him. They'd been together barely a half dozen times during the past two weeks, yet their relationship had grown as though they'd been high-school sweethearts. She was very fond of him, and he of her. There had been no words said to express this fondness, but there was no need for them. A look, a smile, a casual brushing of one hand against the other was all it took.

She smiled as she watched him gamboling in the boiling surf, shouting and waving to her, laughing. He dove into an onrushing wave and disappeared beneath the water. She rose to her feet in sudden alarm when he didn't reappear right away, then breathed a sigh of relief when his head bobbed to the surface.

She snapped the strap of her bathing cap, ran down to the shore and into the surf that flowed over her feet and ankles with foaming fingers. She had never felt as happy as on these afternoons at the beach with Elliot; the bone-white sands of the Southern California beach, the bright blue ocean that stretched to the horizon seemed to blot out the other side of her life completely, the Boomerang Club with its hustling waitresses, Marty and his friends, and even Johnny Kay.

Absorbed in her thoughts, she didn't notice the huge wave gathering to spring at her. She was up to her waist in the cold water when she saw it, and she gasped and stumbled and went under just as the wave sand-bagged her. The water closed over her, shutting off all sound. She surfaced briefly, gasping for breath, spitting out salt water, and then her legs went out from under her and the water closed over her again.

She moved her arms and legs wildly, trying to regain control before her breath ran out. She felt a strong pair of arms grip her and pull her up. The water fell away to sunlight, and she opened her lungs to a breath of air. Elliot was holding her tightly, his face concerned.

"Are you all right?" he asked, holding her securely as another wave came dashing down upon them.

Out of breath, she could only nod gratefully and smile at him. The force of the breaker whirled them like rag dolls, but his arms didn't slacken around her. A moment later, when the boiling sea had calmed, he still held her, and she found that her own arms were around him.

Suddenly it seemed as though they were the only two people in the world, hanging suspended in space and time, each aware only of the other. Their lips met and blended gently, passionately. They pulled each other closer until they could feel their hearts beating in rapid synchronization.

When they finally broke apart, he stared at her for a long moment, and she found herself suddenly aware of the sounds of the surf and the wind and the water moving around their waists and the people crowding the shoreline.

"I—I think we'd better go in," she said.

Wordlessly, he nodded. He put his strong arm around her waist and they walked into shore. On the beach, she lay back on the blanket and closed her eyes until her breath had returned. When she opened them again, Elliot was sitting beside her, still staring.

"You know," he said, breathing a sigh of relief, "you had me worried for a minute out there. You looked like you were having trouble."

"I was. Thanks for saving my life."

"My pleasure. Besides, I couldn't let you get away that easily. I've got some great plans for you. There's a new TV series in the planning stage, and I've been thinking of you for one of the top feature roles. That's one reason I kept coming back to see you at the club."

"Oh, Elliot," she cried excitedly, squeezing his hand.

"Relax," he said, grinning with pleasure at her enthusiasm. "It's still a long way off. We won't even cast for three months. But I think you'll be great for the part I have in mind—a girl who sings and sells sheet music in a New Orleans department store. You'd be in every segment, and it would be a wonderful showcase for you—"

"Oh, Elliot," she said again.

Lois sat, stunned, thinking of what he'd said. And he was doing it for her because he liked her and thought she had talent—and not because he wanted her to go to bed with him. She could feel the emotion building up in her, and suddenly she was in his arms, laughing and crying at once.

"I don't blame you. It's a good break for you," he said, holding her gently. "But I've been watching you closely and I'm sure you can do it."

She nodded understanding. More than ever, her mind was made up—not only by what Elliot had said, but by what he hadn't said. He'd told her one reason he'd come to see her at the club. There were other reasons he didn't have to tell her about—not in words. She knew by the way he held her hand, by the gentleness with which his arm surrounded her, by the look in his gray eyes when he gazed at her. She knew in the same thought that she was getting fond, so very fond, of him, too.

And suddenly even show business was a secondary thing.

"Elliot, I've got to get back to town," she said with sudden resolve. "There's something very important I've got to do."

It wouldn't be easy but it had to be done—for her sake, and for Elliot's. She would tell Marty, once and for all, that she was through.

CHAPTER TEN

"Come on out here and have a drink with me," Marty Masters said as he settled onto the chaise lounge on Lois' veranda.

In his razor-sharp doeskin slacks and gold silk sport shirt, his eyes roaming the burnt almond peaks of the Hollywood Hills, the tanned night club owner resembled a prominent racketeer sunning himself on the Riveria far from Internal Revenue agents.

In fact, Lois decided the description might not be far from wrong. Marty had been involved in some pretty shady deals in other cities, even in cases involving murder. Johnny Kay had told her about some of these, mostly through hints and innuendo, like the story of Marty's ex-partner in Chicago, a man named Hervy Creighton who had been discovered one morning face down in his swimming pool. The death had been termed accidental by drowning, but some people thought it might have been suicide since Marty had been putting the pressure on his partner. Others, who knew both men, had other thoughts which they kept to themselves. In any event, Marty inherited full ownership of the business, as well as a large sum of money from an insurance policy he'd taken out on the partner.

Marty had such a bland, affable, baby-innocent face, even with the mustache, that it was difficult to picture him involved in any real violence, but Lois was certain that many of the stories had a real basis and that if pushed too hard in the wrong direction, Marty would push back, and not gently either.

"Marty, I'd like to have a serious talk with you," she said. "Inside. I don't want the people on the adjoining veranda to hear us."

Marty laughed at her seriousness. He snipped the end of a Romeo y Julieta with a silver cigar cutter that worked like a French guillotine. He was feeling very rich and very important. Lois had helped that, by being nice in a special way to friends who had done him much good.

"I'll be in in a minute, kid. Don't rush me," he said, sipping his drink.

He heard her audible sigh, the sound of her footsteps retreating reluctantly into the apartment. She probably wanted a raise in salary, he decided. They were all like that. When they began at the Boomerang, $200 a week was like heaven to them. A few weeks later when they read publicity items his press agent had planted in various newspapers, and after they'd slept with several men who made six-figure incomes, they decided they were important enough to receive more money.

He looked up to see her standing just inside the doorway, arm folded, lips pursed, an impatient look on her face. There was something on her mind, all right.

"How do you like the cutter?" he inquired casually, holding up the tiny guillotine. "Got it from a guy I'd like you to see when he's back in town. Zundapp Ducatti, one of the richest men in Europe. Involved in autos, oil tankers, planes, banking. Now, *there's* a guy who could take care of your bills, kid. He throws money around like it was confetti on New Year's Eve. I understand he's got an apartment in a dozen cities with a girl living in each one. If this guy likes you, he sets you up like a queen in a palatial apartment, gives you charge accounts, the works. And all you have to do is be handy when he gets into town about once a month. Being tagged as his girl friend is like having an annuity."

"Please come inside, Marty," Lois said. "Now!"

He looked at her, amused by her insistence, the tinge of irritation permeating it. "Sure, kid, sure," he said. He got up heavily from the chair, peered over the railing at a couple of beautiful girls in bikinis sunning themselves around the pool, and carried his drink inside.

"Looks like you have competition here," he grinned at her. "Don't let any of the guys spot those lounge lizards down there by the pool."

He surveyed her full figure in the tight Capris and halter.

"On second thought, maybe you don't have as much competition as I thought." He moved closer to her, put his arms around her waist. "It's been a long time since I took a real close look—"

Coolly, she unwound his arms from her and moved away. He frowned his irritation.

"Okay, kid, what's on your mind? Money?"

She shook her head. "You think anything can be solved by money, don't you? No, it's not money." She went on slowly, deliberately, her voice calm. "I'm grateful for what you've done for me. But I want to call it quits. As of now."

He paused, his jaw hanging open in disbelief. He sat down heavily in a nearby chair. "You what?"

She nodded. "I'm not cut out for this. I thought it would work out, but it's not what I want, after all."

"I understand, kid," Marty said quietly. "We'll take it a little easier for a while. You won't have to see two guys in one day any more. I promise."

She shook her head, wishing he would understand. "It's not just that. I don't want to be a call girl. Period."

He was thoughtful for a moment. "I thought you wanted to break into films and TV?"

"I did," she said.

"Okay. Jim Fritch is going to see that you play a featured role in his movie, isn't he? You've been meeting all kind of useful people you'd never see otherwise. My own personal publicity man is getting you the big build-up. So what the hell are you getting all worked up about? Just because I sent you two guys when you needed money fast? Look, kid, I didn't sic them on to you. You're the one who called me that night, remember?"

"I remember, Marty, but it's not that either. I just don't want any part of it, that's all."

"Suppose you tell me why," Marty said slowly. "You get a sudden attack of morals or something. We talked this thing out, didn't we? This is the way people make contacts, I thought you understood that. This town's full of dolls who look good enough to eat, but there are only so many acting or singing jobs open. If ten girls apply for one job, the one who's best in bed will probably get it"

"It has nothing to do with the morality," she told him. "I'm not worried about that. I came into this with my eyes open; if I couldn't see clearly it was because of the stars in them. I thought I was just sleeping around for show business contacts in the beginning. But I realized after a while that I was becoming just another call girl."

Marty shrugged, but didn't bother to deny it. "Okay, so you're another call girl. So what? I told you I could give you a list of dames in this town who started on a couch and worked their way into leads. Believe me, kid, it can happen to you, too."

"I couldn't care less about show business right now, Marty," she said earnestly. "I know I owe you a lot of money, so I was trying to play the game your way. But I can't any longer. I—I met a man I like very much, and he likes me. He doesn't know what I am, and I don't intend for him to find out. That's why I've got to quit—and now."

"Elliot Jordan?" Marty's face twisted into a sneer. "You think you can do better by being his mistress? What kind of deal's he offering you?"

"I might have known you'd think of that, but it's not like that at all. I'm not planning on shacking up with Elliot. I want to marry him, and I think he wants to marry me. You can see why I have to call it quits. If you want me to continue singing at the club I'll be glad to. But I'm through sleeping with any of your friends. I'm through being a call girl, as of now."

He stared at her for a moment, his face grim. Then, carefully, he lit a cigar and blew smoke into the air.

"It's not that simple, kid," he said. "I've gone out on a pretty big limb for you. I did it because I thought you had something. I still do, and as far as I'm concerned, it was a good investment. But it *was* an investment, and I can't just throw it away. Do you have any idea how much you owe me?"

"I'll pay it back, Marty, I swear—"

Marty took a notebook from his pocket, opened it. "Four grand for the car; seven hundred for clothes; eight hundred for rent on the apartment; a thousand to pay back your aunt; two-fifty for bailing out Johnny Kay—"

"How did you know it was for Johnny?"

"He called me before he called you. I told him I wouldn't lend him another dime, but if you asked for the money I'd let you have it."

She felt the blood rush angrily into her cheeks. "You bastard! You wanted me to ask for money so I'd sleep with your friends!"

He ignored her outburst. "The point is, you owe me a lot of money, and I've got a piece of paper that says so, just as you wanted it, kid." He shrugged and returned the notebook to his coat pocket. "So you see, you just can't walk out the door."

Lois sank into a nearby chair, feeling weak. She knew Marty would bring up the money. "I'll pay you back. It may take you a couple of years, but you'll get paid. Have a heart, Marty, for God's sake. You know I can't go on."

"And I can't afford to have a heart where business is concerned," he said coldly. "Of course, if your friend Elliot Jordan wants to settle it—"

"No," she said quickly. "He mustn't know."

"Okay, then," he said with an air of determination, "there's another way out. I've got a project coming up that'll solve all your problems. You help on this and you can kiss the whole loan good-bye when it's over. I'll just hand over the note you signed and that will be that."

"What project?" she asked suspiciously.

"I want you to come along on a little yacht cruise. A couple of guys I do business with like to do this once a year. They get a ship, invite a few friends and go cruising down to Mazatlan, Acapulco, and then over to Hawaii. It'll take about three weeks. There'll be plenty to eat and drink, and a lot of interesting people to meet. Fishing and sunbathing in the daytime and fun in the evening."

"And you want me to go along as a seagoing call girl, I suppose?" she asked coldly.

"You won't be the only girl on board. There'll be a few others, and you'll all be going as secretaries."

"I thought I made it clear, Marty, I don't want hustling of any kind, and that includes sex on the high seas."

"Lois," Marty said gruffly, "I thought I made it clear to you that I was offering you a way out. You simply spend a couple of weeks on a nice, big comfortable boat—"

"And sleep with every guy on board," Lois interjected angrily, her green eyes flashing.

"—and when you're through with the cruise, you're free as a bird. No debts, no contract, no strings attached. And we part the best of friends. What say?"

Lois was silent a moment. She had no need to consider the matter; her mind had already been made up, and Marty's deal would only get her in deeper. But it was difficult convincing him she meant what she said.

"I can't, Marty. I—well, for one thing, I wouldn't know how to explain being away so long to Elliot."

"Tell him you went off on vacation," Marty snapped irritably. "You're not married to the guy yet, or engaged even. Look, kid, I'm trying to be patient about this, but don't push your luck with me. If you try to pull out of this, I'll have to toss the book at you, and it won't be pleasant for you. I promise."

She clenched her fists helplessly, trying to find words. He got up, went to her, and placed a hand on her shoulder. She shrugged off his touch.

"Look, kid, it won't be so bad," he said. "You'll be away a few weeks—people do take vacations, you know!—and when you come back, your chum Elliot will want to carry you right to church. What's more, there won't be a thing to stop you. As far as the guys on the yacht are concerned, some of them you already know, and the others you'll meet the first night out. We usually get things rolling with a nice wet party."

"Which ends up in the bedroom, I suppose," Lois said sarcastically.

"That's right," Marty said honestly. "What the hell do you expect them to do after dark, play Scrabble?"

"Look, Marty, there are lots of pretty girls in Hollywood who'd buy a deal like that. You ought to be able to round them up without any trouble. Just leave me out of it."

"I couldn't even if I wanted to forget the money you owe me," he said slowly. "Several of the men who are coming specifically asked for you. They've seen you at the Boomerang, and they want you more than anyone else."

"Marty—"

"You'd be a real chump to turn this down, kid. I'm offering you your freedom for a few weeks of your time. Tell you what else I'll do for you. I'll even throw in an extra five hundred to help you buy your trousseau."

"Marty, I *can't!*"

Marty got up, turned to go. His face was a solemn mask. "You'd better change your mind, kid," he said grimly. "I'm not asking you, I'm telling you. I thought you'd see reason, but I'm through playing games with you. You go through with this project, or I'll expect to be paid the money you owe me by the day after tomorrow."

"But I couldn't possibly—"

"And if you don't," he went on, "I'll go to Jordan and try to get it. I'll have you on the S.O.B. list of every night spot in town. Every agent in Hollywood'll know you're a hundred-dollar call girl." His voice softened. "You can avoid wrecking your life, kid, by just co-operating with me for a couple more weeks."

Lois felt numb with the realization that he meant it. She stared at the cold blue eyes and the tight-lipped mouth. The preliminary cat-and-mouse tactics were over, and the cat would surely devour the mouse before it would let the smaller animal go.

"I'll—I'll have to think about it," she said finally.

"Sure, kid," he said expansively. "Take your time. The boat isn't sailing until the end of the week. But I'll expect you on board."

He went to her again, putting his arm around her. "Come on, kid, don't look so damned glum. If you weren't such a ninny you could be the richest girl in Hollywood. I've been around here ten years, and most of the talent available is strictly lousy. Take my word for it, Lois. If you put your mind to it, you could make a fortune in a year in this town, and you'd be fixed for life."

She broke away from him, trying desperately to think of some way she would borrow enough money to buy back her notes from Marty. The sudden ring of the doorbell interrupted her. She walked past Marty to the door and opened it. Johnny was smiling wanly at her.

"Hi," he said, "I was just passing by and I—" He saw Marty. "Oh, I'm sorry. I hope I wasn't interrupting anything."

"I've got to move along anyhow," Marty said gruffly. He went to the door, brushed past Johnny, turned. "Think it over, kid, and let me know tonight."

Chuckling triumphantly, Marty closed the door behind him. Lois stared at the closed door. Then she turned and drove her fist against the wall.

"The bastard!" she cried. "The dirty, filthy, nogood—"

She began to sob helplessly, and Johnny Kay moved to take her in his arms. "Hey, take it easy, honey," he said gently. "It just can't be that bad. Did he give you a hard time?"

She nodded, too upset to speak. She took the handkerchief Johnny handed her and dabbed at her eyes. Slowly, she told him about Marty's ultimatum.

When she was finished, he shrugged. "So what? So you'll do it for another three weeks and get a nice deluxe sea voyage thrown in free. What's your beef? When it's over, you can do what you like. And you'll have a nice bonus to do it with."

She shook her head quickly. "But—"

"Another thing," he said, putting his arm around her waist. "It's not healthy to just walk out on Marty. You ever hear the kids talk about a girl named Franny?"

"The girl who lost control of her car up in the hills?"

"Lost control, hell!" he said. "She drove it off the mountain after Marty told her boy friend how she made money on the side."

Lois closed her eyes and felt a sinking sensation. "Maybe I'd better tell Elliot myself. Before anybody else does."

"You're crazy to even consider it," Johnny said persuasively. "Go on the trip and pay Marty off. Don't be a goon."

His tone irked her. Instead of helping her out of a dilemma, he was just helping Marty push. He was acting like a man who had a stake to protect. Why not? So long as the money came in and he could put the bite on her.

The sudden shrill ring of the phone startled her. She hoped it wasn't one of Marty's friends. She said hello into it, and then smiled her relief.

"Elliot," she said. "Are you coming by this afternoon?"

"I won't be able to make it this afternoon," he said, "but how about after you're through at the club?"

"You mean here at the apartment?"

"Sure. Anything wrong with that? Or are you tied up?"

"No," she said quickly. "I'll be here about two o'clock. Is something up, Elliot. I mean, is there something special?"

"Very special," he said softly. "I've got a surprise for you."

She felt her heart turn over. "What is it? For Pete's sake, don't keep me in suspense."

"It can wait," he said. "Actually, you may not be surprised at all. I've had the feeling that maybe you've been expecting it all along. Anyway, I'll see you at two o'clock."

When he had hung up, she turned to Johnny. "It was Elliot," she said.

"Oh?" Johnny said simply. He was at the bar fixing himself a drink.

"He sounded strange," she said, frowning. "I don't know how, exactly. It was something subtle. Maybe it's just my imagination but—"

Johnny grunted. "He's probably going to pop the question."

"You think he's nervous about asking me?"

Johnny plopped down on the couch and stretched out comfortably. "A man always gets nervous when he asks a woman anything like that; it's traditional."

She ignored his sardonic tone. Her head was bursting with the thought that at last Elliot was going to propose. At last? They'd known each other only a few weeks and yet it seemed like a lifetime. She wondered how she would frame the words when he asked her.

CHAPTER ELEVEN

The night at the club seemed to go with excruciating slowness. No matter when she looked at the illuminated clock behind the bar, the hands seemed to have moved only a few minutes, if at all. She stood in the circle of spotlight and sang to an invisible sea of faces, realizing that this, too, would become a thing of the past. Even if Elliot didn't get her a part in the television series it didn't matter. Her one ambition at the moment was to be Mrs. Elliot Jordan, and nothing else mattered.

She felt a cold chill run through her as she glanced over at the bar and saw Marty staring sullenly at her. He hadn't said anything to her all evening. He was probably waiting for her to make the first move. He didn't know she was going to tell Elliot herself and thus remove any threat he had over her.

Somehow, one-thirty arrived, and Lois stepped down amid the applause and made her way to the bar where Marty was. He removed a cigar from his mouth and looked at her quizzically.

"I'm not going through with it, Marty," she said.

"If you know what's good for you," he said quietly, "you'll change your mind."

He turned and walked away. She was tempted to follow him, but it would only lead to an argument. Besides, she had to meet Elliot at her apartment. That was more important. The business with Marty could come later.

"Can I give you a lift, Johnny?" she asked him.

"I want to do some work on my own stuff for a while," he said. "I'll grab a cab. Thanks anyway."

When she went out into the parking lot, she felt a new sense of freedom. It was as though she were leaving it and all it represented behind her, and she could feel her pulse quicken perceptibly at the thought of Elliot coming to her apartment to propose.

She had barely time to change into something less formal before the doorbell rang. She ran to the door, threw it open. Elliot stood in the hallway and stared thoughtfully at her. She wondered if all men about to propose looked so deadly serious.

"Wonderful timing," she said gaily. "Come in."

"Thanks," he said.

He walked past her into the living room. She was surprised that he made no effort to kiss her.

"Would you like a drink?" she asked him.

"Thanks," he said. "I've already had quite a few, but I could use another. How about Scotch on the rocks?"

"Coming right up," she said, and went to the bar to get it.

It wasn't like Elliot to drink, but then he'd probably never proposed before and was nervous and thought he could loosen his tongue with alcohol. She motioned awkwardly toward the couch and they sat down. An enigmatic smile seemed glued to his face like a theatrical mask.

"You're certainly in a strange mood," she said, trying to keep her tone somewhere between banter and earnestness. "You're either hugging a secret or nursing a problem. What's this thing you were going to tell me?"

He gazed at her for a moment, his eyes roaming along her body. Then he put down the glass and reached out for her, pulling her to him and kissing her on the mouth, smearing his lips wetly against hers. He took her hair in his hands and shoved her head back.

"Elliot," she said, trying to catch her breath. "Wait a minute."

"Oh, I'm sorry," he said with exaggerated politeness. "Am I too rough?" He released her and leaned back and studied her body once more. "You know, I've wanted to go to bed with you since that first time I saw you at the Boomerang. You were a waitress then, and you were wearing one of those skimpy red costumes that looked like it was sprayed on your beautiful behind. And there were those gorgeous breasts nearly falling out, and the luscious legs in black net stockings. Yeah, I really wanted to go to bed with you."

She stared at him, puzzled by his tone and the turn of conversation. "I—I thought you wanted to tell me something," she said nervously.

"I'm telling it to you now, Lois," he said calmly. "I want to go to bed with you. And I don't want any discount either. I'll pay the full tab."

Automatically, her hand leaped out and struck his face. He put his hand against his cheek and smiled.

"My, you've got a temper," he said. "What are you getting so sore about? I made you a civil proposition, didn't I?"

"Elliot, I'm sorry," she said, "I didn't mean—"

"That's all right," he said. "Don't give it another thought.'

He reached out for her again and pulled her to him. He began kissing her neck and the cleavage of her breasts. Suddenly, he pushed his fist into the top of her dress, and she felt a wad of paper between her breasts.

"That should make us friends," he said proudly. "Those are two fifties, baby. Your standard rate, according to what the boys tell me. It's a little more than I can afford, but then I understand you're a special girl. You not only screw, you sing, too; which puts you in a class above the regular whores. Do you have any other talents, or does it cost even more money to find out?"

"Elliot," Lois said helplessly, "please let me explain."

"I didn't come here to talk," he said. "I want what I paid for, and it's going to be worth every cent for the education. Why should I be the only guy on the Strip who doesn't know every freckle on your backside!"

He picked her up in his arms like a sack of potatoes and carried her into the bedroom, ignoring her pleadings and her frantic struggles to get away. He dumped her on the bed and began pushing her dress up over her hips.

"Elliot, don't, please," she begged. "You're drunk. You don't know what you're doing."

"Not that drunk, baby," he said. "I know *exactly* what I'm doing."

He forced the dress roughly over her shoulders and head and threw it on the floor. She could smell the whiskey on his breath as he leaned over her.

"Please, Elliot." Tears of frustration were stinging her eyes, running down her cheeks. "Let me explain. I was going to tell you tonight. Honest, I was."

"What's there to explain?" he asked matter-of-factly, as he clutched at her brassiere. "My girl friend just happens to be one of the highest paid call girls in Hollywood. Maybe I ought to be grateful for all the free time you've given me. There's nothing else to explain, nothing to apologize for. Maybe I should apologize to the guy who gave me your phone number and told me to ask for Lois. He was doing me a favor and I didn't realize it. The last thing he said before I hit him was: 'She's a little expensive but she's the best lay in L.A.' He thought the rime was so good he repeated it: 'the best lay in L.A.' Come to think of it, it isn't too bad. If he hadn't taken me by surprise it might have sounded better. Now, hold still and let me see if he's right."

He turned her on her stomach and fumbled with the hooks of the bra. She felt weak, all resistance drained from her. It had all gone so wrong, so terribly wrong, and she felt sick and ashamed for being what she was—and sorry for the way Elliot had found out about her. She buried her head in the pillow, crying into it. Through the sound of her own weeping, she was aware of the bitterness in his tone.

"I was going to ask you to marry me," he said. "I spent two hours yesterday trying to get you a ring. My God, I must have been out of my mind. You probably almost died laughing at me. Here I saw you two or three times a week and I never tried to lay you. You must have thought I was a eunuch. I wondered why I got those looks from the other girls at the Boomerang whenever I went down to hear you. They must have thought I was the prize jerk of Hollywood. Me, I was in seventh heaven because I thought you loved me."

She turned a tear-stained face from the pillow. "I do love you, Elliot. For God's sake, believe me. I started all that before I ever met you. And because of you I was quitting it. I told Marty I wasn't going to do it any more, that I was going straight from here on in. The only reason I did it in the first place was because he told me it was the only way to get ahead—and like a fool I believed him!"

He stared at her, his face a mask of scorn. "You did it to get ahead! You think that excuses you for making a damned fool of me, for screwing guys all over town who tell me about it after I tell them I'm crazy about you? Funny you didn't think about telling me before I found out. Oh, I didn't just take this one fellow's word for it, I checked around. I heard all about you and Tony Formio."

His voice had risen and Lois was afraid the neighbors would hear them. If only he would listen to her, let her explain.

"Please, Elliot," she pleaded. "Don't shout."

"Sure," he said quietly. "Sorry. Why should I waste your time by talking? Let's get on to the main event. Let's see if Tony Formio and I have the same taste."

He took hold of her panties—she moved away on the bed, trying to elude his grasp.

"Stop it, Elliot!" she said. "I don't want to. Not like this. You're drunk, hurt and angry—and I don't blame you. I want you to make love to me because I love you, but not like this, not tonight."

"The hell you say, sweetie," he said, tugging roughly at the panties. "I paid, didn't I? Let's stop the discussion and see a little action."

Something in his voice—the matter-of-factness of it, condemning her without letting her at least try to explain—enraged her suddenly. He wasn't Elliot any more, he was a stranger, and she didn't want him to touch her. She began to kick furiously at him with both legs, but his hand took the thin material of her panties and ripped them from her. He fought her with a fury that astonished her, pinning down each leg as it flew toward his chest.

"A little spitfire, huh?" he said. "Good. I love spitfires. Tony and the others were right, you've got good breasts, nice hips, everything they said—every detail about you is right." He began to remove his clothes as she squirmed against him, gasping for breath beneath his weight. "Is this standard practice, or just the hundred-dollar job?"

Lois had no desire to reason with him; both of them were beyond that. She'd felt sorry for him, but now she was angry and she hated him with an intensity she had never known for anyone.

"Get away from me!" she yelled, pummeling him with both fists. "Get away from me. You're as bad as the others! "

"Why not?" he shouted back at her. "Any reason you should discriminate just because I was once in love with you? My money's as good as theirs, isn't it?" He grabbed her hair and forced her head back. "Isn't it? Answer me, you goddamn slut!"

She felt as though her neck were being broken, as though he were trying to tear her hair out by the roots. His perspiring body was heavy on hers, crushing the breath from her. The smell of whiskey on his breath made her feel sick. Tears of anger and humility stung her eyes.

"Yes," she cried. "Yes, yes, yes!"

In a moment he was naked, embracing her, putting all his anger and fury into making love to her. She clawed at him with her nails, but he pinned her against the bed, holding her arms, bearing heavily on her so she could hardly move. At the instant of possession the fight drained from her and she could only turn her sobbing face away from him, just wishing it were over and she could be alone.

He made love to her coldly, drunkenly, and her body became as limp as a rag as he used it. Afterward, she lay back on the bed and stared unemotionally at the ceiling.

Elliot stood up and stared down at her. He dressed quickly and left the room without a word. She didn't look at him.

She heard the front door open and close, and a silence drifted back on her she felt as though a door had closed on everything she had ever wanted from life. She had hated him while he made love to her. Now she felt only sorrow. Sorrow for what he must have gone through when he found out about her from someone else, from perhaps a dozen someone elses. Her thoughts were calm now, and she felt no emotion.

In a few minutes, she rose and went out into the living room. She mixed herself a strong Scotch, sat down and sipped it slowly, not thinking about what had happened or about what she was going to do, just letting the stunned sensation wear off.

It was ironic that Marty's threat to tell Elliot was now useless. Elliot knew everything, so it didn't matter what happened on the yacht. Maybe Johnny was right about her going. The cruise would enable her to settle her account with Marty, and afterwards she could fly to New York or Chicago and get a job and try to forget Elliot, Marty, the Boomerang, everything.

She hated the idea of calling Marty and eating crow. It galled her to think of groveling before him, of seeing his triumphant smirk. For several minutes she stared numbly at the phone, unable to make herself lift the receiver. When she finally did pick it up, she found herself dialing the number of the Boomerang and then asking for Johnny.

"Johnny, I had to talk to someone," she said when he answered. "You're the only one in town I can trust. There are two and a half million people in L.A. and yet sometimes I feel like I'm living on the moon."

"It's a pretty cold town," Johnny agreed. "Have you decided what you're going to do?"

"That's why I called you."

She told him what had happened with Elliot.

"I'm sorry, Lois," he said when she'd finished. "Anyway, this means that by taking the cruise now, you've got nothing to lose—and a hell of a lot to gain, your freedom."

"I know," she said. "But I can't get myself to call Marty. He said he wanted to know tonight, but I just don't know if I can go through with it, Johnny."

"Sure you can," he assured her. "This is a way to get Marty off your back. After the cruise, you'll be as free as a bird and you can do whatever you want without having to worry about hurting someone's feelings or being in debt." He paused briefly, then said, "Tell you what. Let me tell Marty for you. I'll let him know you're doing him a favor by going on the cruise and he damn well better be grateful. I'll say you'll be ready whenever he says, okay?"

She hesitated for only an instant. "Okay," she said, and felt relieved for having made the decision.

"That's a good girl," Johnny said soothingly. "Now, why don't you get to bed and have some rest. I'll call you tomorrow and tell you the details."

He hung up and looked across the desk at Marty's grinning face.

"It's all set, boss," Johnny said. "She'll be ready whenever you are."

"Good," Marty said. "I'd have been in a hell of a spot if she conked out on me now. I told everybody she was coming. I'll have a check for you tomorrow, but I expect you to deliver her in Long Beach at six o'clock Saturday. Got that?"

"Got it."

"Tell her what to pack and wear. And look, stay with her. I don't want any more trouble. I got too many other worries to put up with tantrums from a stupid chippie."

"I'll stay with her, don't worry. And—uh—Marty, can you make that check an extra hundred? I really need it. My wife's been bugging me for more money."

Marty hesitated, frowning. Then he said, "Okay, another hundred. But you'd better stay sober while I'm gone or that'll be the last buck you ever see, from me or anyone else in this town."

Johnny paused at the door. "That was pretty smart of you, Marty," he commented. "Sending that guy over to spill the beans to Elliot."

"Sure it was," Marty barked. "It's the only way to survive in this damned jungle. You've got to play the angles. Now get the hell out of here. I've got a new singer coming in for an audition in a few minutes. A real doll, with magnum-size jugs. I don't think our customers are even going to miss little Lois!"

CHAPTER TWELVE

The Greyhound lay quietly at anchor in the big marina at Long Beach harbor. In the late afternoon sunlight, the beautifully sleek yacht, its rakish lines etched against the golden sky, was like a painting of a sea captain's dream of heaven.

Despite her nervousness, Lois was swept by a feeling of excitement. She turned to Johnny who was behind the wheel of the Thunderbird, parked beside the water.

"It's beautiful," she said. "But why do they call it the *Greyhound?* It's white, not gray. And who is Night Keene? What an odd name."

Johnny grinned at her enthusiasm. "Night Keene is one of the biggest dog track owners in the country. He got the nickname 'Night' because he used to boast all the time that he never made a nickel until it was dark. Most of his money is tied up in dog tracks, bowling alleys, equipment for tracks, stuff like that. Of course, now he's involved in construction and other fields, too. His favorite dog's a greyhound, so he calls his yacht that."

She looked out at the craft again. An afternoon breeze had sprung up and was blowing in from the ocean, bringing with it the sound of the waves lapping at the rocks beyond the marina, the resonant clang of a buoy, the cold salt smell of the sea. The yacht was a beautiful thing, but what it represented was not beautiful—three weeks of giving her body to strangers. She tried not to think of that, but of what would come after those three weeks—freedom from Marty and from her financial troubles.

She recalled an old saying: if rape is inevitable, relax and enjoy it. It was supposed to be funny. Well, this was rape. It was inevitable. It wasn't funny.

"The launch should be out here in a few minutes," Johnny said, glancing at his watch. "You all set?"

"Sure," she said, forcing a wan smile. The closer the time came for her to leave, the more she dreaded it. "I'm supposed to be a secretary, and this is a business trip, is that it?"

"Right. You might call it a floating board meeting. There'll be about a dozen men on the yacht, all of whom are involved in some way with Keene. They're going to Mexico and Hawaii to inspect building sites, oil leases and other stuff. There'll be some business meetings daily, of course, and some reports and correspondence and cables to send out to New York, L.A. and Chicago. The secretaries are supposed to handle the clerical details. By rigging this up as a business trip, these guys can take it off their income taxes."

"Well, I'm glad there'll be some real secretaries on tap," she said. "Oh, look, there's the launch." She turned to Johnny. "You still haven't told me what arrangements are being made. Do I have my own cabin or do I move in with somebody."

"I really don't know," Johnny said uneasily. "I'm sure Marty'll fill you in on the details when you get on board."

"I wish you were coming with us," she said wistfully.

"Me, too. No such luck. You have to be pretty big in the money department to get in on this one. It isn't any bargain tour, you know. I could live like a king for months on what these guys'll pay for this cruise. You should come out of it with a nice little bonus."

He looked away, embarrassed, and pretended to watch the launch bearing down on them across the water. "Which reminds me. I wonder if—"

She smiled and opened her purse. "Will forty help?"

He grinned and took the money. "Everything helps. Thanks, and *bon voyage*."

She kissed him affectionately on the mouth. "Take care of yourself, Johnny. Try to work on those arrangements, the ones you played for me. They could turn into something real great for you." She took his arm firmly. "And I don't want to find you sick when I get back. Stay off the sauce. Promise?"

"Sure," he said.

She got out of the car as a seaman came up to take her bags. She started to follow when Johnny called her name. She turned and saw him coming toward her. He stopped, trying to find words.

"When you get back, Lois," he said, "maybe—well, maybe you and I could—what I mean is, my divorce is going to be final in just a couple of months. You and I could get married, maybe go to New York or Chicago and work together there as a team."

For a moment she stood and looked at his thin, gaunt face. A sea breeze was playing havoc with his dark, unruly hair. Standing there waiting for her answer, he looked more lost and forlorn than ever. Impulsively, she moved up to him and kissed him.

"Oh, Johnny, Johnny," she said. She looked into his sad, dark eyes. "Thanks, Johnny, not only for asking me but for wanting me. The way I feel now, well … it's like getting a shot in the arm just to be asked. But I'm all mixed up inside. You're the best friend I have. I think if you hadn't talked to me on the phone after Elliot left—I just don't know what would have happened. But as for marriage, we're too much alike. We're both dreamers, unrealistic, running along a make-believe rainbow after a pot of gold that isn't there. I think we need different people."

"We'd be good for each other, Lois," he insisted. "And I'd really stick to the music with you around. I swear to God I would.

I'd do anything you asked. Give up drinking, move anywhere you say." He took her in his arms and held her close. "I need you, Lois. Without you around, I'll be drifting until I'm fifty, if I last that long. If we can get together, try to make something new out of our lives, I can do anything, and I know it. And one thing you know: no matter what you've done, or who you've stayed with, I think you're the tops. I mean that. I'd always feel that way."

"We've got to leave now, miss," a voice yelled from the end of the pier where the launch was waiting.

"You don't have to say anything now, honey," Johnny said quickly. "Think about it on the trip, and I'll be waiting for you when you get back."

"All right, Johnny," she said softly, touched by his proposal and his need.

She turned and walked down the pier, occasionally looking back and waving to him as he stood beside the pink Thunderbird. He was still there when the launch drew up to the Greyhound's starboard side, but then her attention was commanded by the appearance of Marty who greeted her from the deck.

"Hi, kid," he said, giving her a hand as she climbed the ladder, "welcome on board."

He looked very nautical in his blue trousers and light blue sport shirt, and he even had a yachting cap on his head. She gave him what she hoped was a pleasant smile, but she couldn't help feel trapped now that she was on the boat. Once the anchor lifted, there would be no way back.

Marty led her to her cabin. The size and luxury of it left her speechless. If she hadn't known she was on a ship, she would have thought herself in a de luxe hotel. The custom-built furniture of polished mahogany, the large bed, the expensive couch and chairs, reminded her more of Jim Fritch's rooms at the Beverly Hilton than a cabin on a yacht.

"Like it, kid?" Marty asked, puffing on his cigar.

Lois nodded. "I had no idea anybody could live like this at sea."

Marty opened a wall cabinet and took out a cut-glass decanter of whiskey and an ice bucket. "This is nothing," he said, as he mixed them two drinks. "Wait till you see Night Keene's place. It looks like something out of a Warner Brothers movie. Let's drink to a profitable voyage."

They sat and drank quietly. The yacht was stirring gently, the water lapping at its side. There was the sound of footsteps, an occasional plaintive cry of a seagull. Then the rattle of chains as the anchor came up from the marina floor.

"Everybody must be aboard," Marty said. "All right, kid, let's get down to business. The setup's like this. This is, supposedly, a business trip, and actually part of it is. We'll have some business meetings during the mornings, and you may have to take some cables to the radio man and maybe do a little typing. Just enough so it looks right, you know what I mean?"

"I can't type very well," Lois said.

Marty laughed. "Neither can any of the other girls. Just fake it enough so it looks right to the crew. They may guess the girls weren't picked for their typing or shorthand, but all we want them to do is guess. During the rest of the day you'll be on your own. Some of the guys may do a little fishing when we get down around Ensenada, La Paz or Mazatlan, but most of them are on board to have a party."

The powerful motors of the yacht vibrated through the room, then died to a soft hum as the boat began to move. They went to the porthole and watched the shore recede. Lois looked to the spot where she'd left the car and Johnny, but neither of them were in sight.

"Well, we're off," Marty announced.

He went to fix them fresh drinks. He showed her the route the ship would follow, using a wall map hanging nearby. The first stop, in a few days, was La Paz on the Baja California peninsula. They could go across the Gulf of California to Mazatlan and spend a couple of days. Then to Acapulco, and from there across the Pacific to Hawaii.

"It sounds wonderful," Lois said, trying desperately to convince herself that it was. Except that she couldn't help thinking of what would be happening during that long, long journey.

"It is," Marty said enthusiastically. "Now tonight there'll be a little get-acquainted party after dinner. You'll meet a lot of guys. Be nice to all of them. But don't go into anyone's cabin unless I say so. That clear?"

She nodded. "When do I get my note, Marty?"

"When we get back to L.A. There's no problem, kid. Just cooperate and we'll be square when it's over. I can even guarantee you a couple of grand over and above our little debt. How does that sound?"

"A couple of thousand dollars?" she asked surprised. "I don't get it. I know these men are wealthy, but you think they'll pay that much."

Marty chuckled. "Oh, they'll pay plenty, all right. But I'm paying you the extra two grand to do something special for me, something more important than sleeping with these guys."

"Like what?" she asked, suspicious and puzzled.

"I'll show you." He went to a bureau and unlocked a drawer. From it he took a tiny leather case, which he unzipped, and drew out a miniature tape recorder.

"Now give me your purse," he commanded.

She gave him her purse and watched silently while he put the recorder inside. She wondered why Johnny had insisted she bring along her large purse, and now she realized why, although she still couldn't fathom the purpose of it. Marty closed her purse, put it on a nearby table, and said a few words in a normal tone about what a lovely trip it was going to be. Then he opened the purse again and played back what he'd said.

Lois was starting to understand, and she didn't like it. "What do you expect me to do with that?" she asked quietly.

"What do you think? I don't expect you to record seagull cries. I want you to turn it on when you see one of these guys and get him to talk about himself, his family, his business. And especially get him to tell you what he wants to do to you—in vivid detail."

She flushed angrily. "I won't do it, Marty. You're not going to make me a party to blackmail!"

"Lower your voice, damn you," he barked. And in a softer tone, he added, "Now, let's not fly off the handle. I'm not going to blackmail them. All I want is to have something on ice that'll— uh—influence them in my favor. And it won't be just sex. These men have a lot of business secrets they may spill to you, things I might like to know. The sex talk is just insurance to help them play along."

"No," she said firmly. "The only deal I agreed to was to go along on this sea orgy and sleep with anyone you say. Blackmail wasn't part of the agreement, and I'm not going to do it. Count me out."

Marty's face turned grim. He shook his head. "I can't count you out, kid," he said slowly. "You're in it up to your neck. But I'll tell you what I'll do to make the pill sweeter; I'll make your bonus three grand. Okay?"

"It doesn't matter about the money. I just don't want any part of it."

"Five grand, then," Marty said in a hard voice, "and that's my top offer."

"I said no, Marty!" she insisted, irritated that he wouldn't believe her. "I may be a whore, but I'm not a filthy blackmailer."

Marty's hand leaped out and struck her full on the cheek, and she reeled back in hurt and surprise, a hand to her stinging cheek. Marty's face was livid with rage.

"I said lower your voice, kid, and I meant it. I don't like temperamental women. I can take just so much and then I let go. Don't get me sore again, kid. I won't be so gentle next time."

At the doorway he turned back to her. "Dinner's in twenty minutes. Wear something that really shows off those lovely jugs of yours." He paused. "About the other, just make up your mind that you're going through with it. Otherwise, I'll have to persuade you. It would be a shame to smash up that pretty face of yours."

CHAPTER THIRTEEN

Lois would have enjoyed the dinner much more if the men at the table had not kept undressing her boldly with their eyes. As Marty had suggested, she wore a dress that was very tight and cut very low in front.

The cook had made the most delicious curried shrimp she had ever eaten, and there was an excellent French Chablis to wash it down. The cabin was festooned with gay flowers and Japanese lanterns, and the guests sitting at the several tables looked as though they were enjoying a luxury cruise.

She saw Binnie as soon as she walked into the room. The redhead was wearing a jersey sheath that looked as though it had been sprayed on her voluptuous breasts and hips; she looked up and glared coldly from the other end of the cabin.

The other five girls were strangers to her. They had in common a kind of flashy sensuality that one came to expect in Marty's girls. They had the kind of curves that made men turn around wherever they walked and an inviting smile seemingly frozen on their pretty faces. Lois wondered how long it would have taken before she would be described in that fashion—if it wasn't already true.

The dozen men in the room had something in common, too. They all looked like men who were used to making a lot of money and running their own shows. Most of them were in their late forties of early fifties. Many of them were balding and fat, and there was not a shrinking violet in the bunch. They leered outright at the girls as they troweled the sauce-drenched food into their mouths and paused between sips of wine to engage in knee-fondling conversation with the girls.

When she entered the dining room, the first one she saw was Marty, grinning and acting very congenial. Of the men, she recognized Si Bender, the accountant, and Bert Ralston, the trucking company man; both of the men smiled and waved to her.

Marty introduced her to everyone as one of the secretaries. The men immediately focused their eyes on her, measuring her breasts and hips as though she were up for auction. Then Marty led her to a small table at which two men were seated.

"I want you to meet Night Keene and Zundapp Ducatti," Marty said affably.

Lois smiled and nodded to them. Ducatti got to his feet, and Keene reluctantly followed suit.

Night Keene was a tall, thin man with an aquiline nose and cold china-blue eyes. She could see the heavy drinker's network of thin red lines on his nose.

Ducatti was obviously a European. His round face and bulbous nose reminded her of the fat, jolly, middle-aged men who tipped her heavily at the Boomerang and occasionally pinched her bottom. His brown eyes were very warm, and his big cavalryman's mustache made him look like an Italian general. He spoke quickly in a foreign accent as he squeezed her hand, and Lois found herself liking him.

"So this is the beautiful Lois at last," he said, his eyes fixing hers in a way that shut out everyone else. He turned to Marty. "Marty, Marty, why didn't you introduce her to me the last time?"

"Because you were flying to Paris the day I met her," Marty said. "Relax, you'll be seeing a lot of her for the next few weeks."

"Yes," Ducatti said, eying her shrewdly. "I want to see a lot of her."

"Not tonight you aren't, Zundie," Night Keene interjected, his tone blurred. "This is my boat and I get first crack at bat. Any objection?"

His sharp, belligerent tone surprised Lois. He sounded like a small boy warning others off his hill.

But Zundapp laughed good-naturedly and slapped Night on the back. "Let's not be foolish, Night old friend. I do too much business to annoy you."

"And don't you forget it, Zundie," Keene said, covering his tone with a wan smile. He turned to Lois and said, "I liked your looks the minute I saw you, honey." He squeezed her knee, firmly, affectionately. "I don't like small girls. I told Marty you had to come when he showed me your picture."

The dinner proceeded quietly for the next hour as immaculately-uniformed stewards served them. Under Night Keene's urging she drank several glasses of Chablis and champagne with the desert, a mouth-watering soufflé made with Grand Marnier. She didn't like Keene, and she was distressed that she would have to see him later that evening. She would much rather have gone off with Ducatti, who was at least warm and friendly.

When the dinner was over, the room became flooded with dance music pouring from speakers in various corners of the room. The stewards cleared the tables and then removed many of them to make room, brought in trays of caviar, pâté de foie gras and English biscuits which they set on a huge sideboard next to numerous bottles of champagne cooling in buckets.

The room went dark, and spotlights came on from various parts of the room, with colored discs revolving in front of the lenses, changing the lighting from red to blue to green to orange. It was soft, exotic lighting and intended to be romantic.

She found herself dancing with Zundapp Ducatti. The
European was surprisingly nimble for a man of his girth, and an
excellent dancer.

"I wish I could have you tonight, darling," he whispered in
her ear. "But what can I do?" He screwed up his face in a gesture
of helplessness that made her laugh. "As Night so firmly pointed
out, this is his boat and I am only a guest. *Noblesse oblige.*"

Binnie was being wheeled around the floor by a huge man
who held her in a bear hug. A very young blonde was dancing
with a bald man who crushed himself against her breasts in a
way that left nothing to the imagination. His hands kept slipping
down to squeeze her buttocks and she, obviously embarrassed,
kept discouraging his eagerness. She threw Lois a look of helpless
frustration, and Lois retaliated with a look of sympathy, grateful that Zundapp wasn't making any obvious overtures with his
hands and body.

"Poor Alfred," Zundapp said, glancing at the young girl's
partner. "He's married to a fright, who's not merely a hag but an
unpleasant one. When he comes on one of these cruises, he runs
amok. It always embarrasses me to see anyone show naked desire
that way, so desperately. But he's not alone. Look over there."

Lois turned to see a short, stocky man trying to kiss the deep
cleavage of the girl he was dancing with. The girl kept laughing and moving her breasts just out of reach of his eager lips.
The man's desire and short-windedness had made beads of sweat
break out on his forehead. Finally, in desperation, he grabbed the
girl's dress and plunged his hand inside. The girl winced with
pain as the man roughly caressed her, but she made no movement to get away.

Nearby, Binnie was being kissed by Si Bender, who had
backed her into a corner and was giving her no opportunity for
escape.

A dark-haired girl she didn't know was sitting on Bert Ralston's lap, and he was holding her very close, running his hand up and down her leg.

Another girl was standing on a table singing with the music, while a circle of admirers sat around her gazing up in admiration.

The music was almost drowned out by the lupine shouts of the half-drunken men as they danced, embraced or fed the girls. There were a few brief skirmishes as one man tried to dance with another man's partner, but no ill feelings were apparent. Marty stood on the sidelines, watching with great amusement.

Lois was passed from one dancer to another, though she tried to stay with Zundapp Ducatti as much as possible. Once, she danced with Alfred and she felt sick beneath the obvious onslaught of his body and hands.

Her partners stopped every so often to force drinks on her, and though she drank them it seemed as though everyone else was getting much drunker than she. She felt giddy and she refused to have any more. Binnie and the young blonde seemed afraid of refusing the profferred drinks, and it wasn't long before both were staggering across the floor trying to dodge the multicolored circles of light that moved beneath their feet.

Suddenly, a shapely redhead with green eyes and a tiny pert nose gave out with a piercing rebel yell. She turned angrily on her partner and shouted: "I'll show you who's got the best chest on board, damn you!"

She began to pull her dress over her head and everybody crowded around to stare at her. As her skirt moved up past her hips, there was a wave of heavy, raucous laughter and a wolf whistle. The redhead wasn't wearing any lingerie under the dress.

"Hey, you ain't going to let her get away with that crack, are you?" Bert Ralston demanded of the dark-haired girl beside him. "I'm voting for you, honey. Let's show her you've got a pair that'll make her look like a boy! " He began unzipping the girl's dress from the rear, while she stood very still, a drunken smile on her face.

"I got a better idea," another man yelled. "Let's make it a contest. I'll give a hundred bucks to the best chest in the room. Anybody sweeten the kitty?"

"Count me in," another man chmed n.

"Me, too."

In a moment every man in the room was offering to add to the cash prize.

"Wait a minute, though," Si Bender said. "Let's pick candidates and the guy who picks the winner takes her home later. If there are two or more they can either draw cards or take turns."

It was agreed to, and several of the girls were herded into the center of the floor, too drunk to resist or even to care as the men eagerly undressed them. The young blonde, her eyes wide with fear, hurried to Lois' side. She introduced herself as Harriet Swanson.

"I don't like this, Lois," she said. "I don't want to be a part of any orgy, and it looks like this one could turn out that way. I know a girl who got sent to the hospital after something like this. They just go nuts with all that liquor in them."

Lois turned as Zundapp Ducatti called her name. "I take it you don't want to enter the contest?" he asked blandly.

She nodded. "I'd like to get out of here."

"So would I," Harriet said quickly. "I have an idea this party's going to get too rough in a few minutes."

"You're right," Ducatti agreed. "I am not fond of orgies myself. I had no idea they were going to pull this sort of thing. Why don't you both come with me."

He led them to a door at the far end of the cabin as the other girls continued their stripping, the men cheering them loudly.

"What's the matter with them?" Binnie yelled suddenly. She stood naked from the waist, her large breasts jutting proudly in the dim light. "You got something to hide, Lois? You wearing foam rubber under that dress?"

The other half-nude girls shouted jeers at them. "Come on, Lois. Come on, Harriet. Be a sport!"

The men chimed in with calls of encouragement.

"Hey," Night Keene's sullen voice dominated the room, "where the hell you think you're going with Lois, Zundie? I told you she's my date!" He turned irritably to Marty, who came rushing up. "Didn't you fix her up with me tonight?"

"Sure, Night, sure," Marty said, "there's a small misunderstanding. Just a minute."

He walked quickly to where Lois was standing and pulled her to one side, squeezing her arm with a vengeance.

"What are you trying to do, queer everything?" he demanded angrily. "You stay with Keene tonight, understand?"

She winced as his fingers increased their pressure on her arm. She stared, frightened, at him, wanting to run to her cabin and lock herself in. But she could only nod, speechless.

"Look, I asked you a question," he said. "I don't want to ruin that pretty puss of yours, but I will if you don't start co-operating."

"All right," she said. "You're hurting me."

"This is nothing to what'll happen to you if you act funny again." He pulled her with him to Keene's side. "She's just a little tired, Night, but not that tired. You want her to stick around till the party's over, she'll be delighted. Won't you, kid?"

"Yes," Lois said quickly as Marty squeezed her arm again.

Night Keene smiled coldly; his icy gaze raking her body. "Hell, I don't want to share that view with anybody. Let's go right now."

Marty released her and Night took over, ushering her out of the cabin into the narrow corridor. Behind them, the party resumed, and Lois could see Marty reprimanding Harriet for her attempt to escape. She moved stiffly ahead of Night as he directed her down the corridor.

"My place or yours?" he said, uttering the classic line that would have been funny if it hadn't been so personal.

"Mine," she said sullenly. What did it matter, anyway? She was only sorry now that she hadn't had more to drink. At least, she would have been too blind to know or care what was happening to her.

She entered her cabin, switched on the lights. Night Keene followed her and locked the door behind him. She turned to face him, and she almost gasped at the ferocious, animal look on his face.

"All right," he said coldly. "Take it off. Fast!"

She began to undo the buttons on her dress. It was not fast enough for him. He strode to her and ripped the buttons out of their holes.

"I haven't got all night," he barked.

He pushed her down on the bed roughly and told her to stretch her legs. Then he ripped each stocking off. She reddened and tried to move away.

"You're ruining my best stockings," she complained. "Here, let me take them off."

"Shut up," he said, "and keep those legs high."

She sat up angrily. "No!" she said defiantly. "Just who the hell do you think you are?"

He slapped her face, hard. "That tell you who I am?" he said triumphantly.

She fell back on the bed, her senses reeling from the impact of the blow. It had stung at first, but then it held a disturbing numbness. Her mind became a frantic whirlpool as he knelt beside her on the bed and began to claw at her bra and panties without another word. Her blood ran cold as his rough hands grabbed at her flesh, and she jumped off the bed and out of his reach.

"Where do you think you're going, whore?" he demanded. "Get down there on the bed where you belong."

He pulled a money clip from his pocket and peeled off several bills and tossed them to the floor.

"That'll pay for any bruises," he said. "Now stop running around and get over here."

When she froze, terrified, against the wall, he rose. She took one look at his bloodshot eyes, his furious face, and ran for the door. When she discovered it was locked, she screamed. She felt his hand on her naked shoulder, spinning her around. She caught the fast blur of his moving hand, and she felt the palm of it strike her cheek once more.

"Go on, yell," he said. "Nobody will hear you. And if they did, they wouldn't care. What the hell are you screaming for, anyway? You're getting paid for it, aren't you?"

He took some more bills and threw them in her direction.

"Come on," he said.

"Please don't beat me," she begged, as he moved toward her, the cords standing out in his throat.

"I'm just warming up, kiddo," he said, laughing at her.

He caught her in his arms and pulled her over to the bed, throwing her down on her stomach. Then he began to paddle her naked behind with his palm, shouting curses and laughing all the while. She began to sob with pain, begging him to stop. But he paid her no attention. Her cries made him angry, and he turned her over and began to slap and beat her mercilessly. The room rocked, teetered, she felt dizzy—and then everything blacked out.

When she awakened the next morning Night Keene was gone.

Scattered about the room were seven fifty-dollar bills.

CHAPTER FOURTEEN

The girls were eating alone in the dining room when Lois reached it. The number one topic was the previous night's beauty contest, which Harriet had won.

"She wound up with Rodney Garris," one of the girls said, laughing. "He makes love like a halfback heading into a scrimmage."

The girls greeted her warmly. Only Binnie ignored her. In the gray morning light, their glamour was gone. As they introduced themselves, Lois couldn't help noting that all looked tired as if they were suffering from too much wine and lack of sleep.

"Welcome to the Boomerang Club," Alice Turandel, the plump redhead said with a grin. "So you're Marty's latest star attraction. I wondered who you were last night, but I was too busy fighting for my honor to ask. You were hired after Binnie, weren't you?"

"That's right," Binnie said, "and the knife she put in my back is still dripping blood."

"Don't take that attitude, Binnie," Mavis Gordon, the brunette said. "If it hadn't been Lois, it would be someone else, so what's the sense in getting sore at her?"

"Because she connived the whole rotten thing," Binnie said. "And all that baloney about being an artist instead of a call girl. I noticed it didn't take her long to get invited to one of these seagoing mattress parties!"

"Listen, Binnie," Lois said carefully, "I told you I had nothing to do with getting your job. You can believe that or not, but don't make any more accusations unless you want a repeat of what happened the first time you tried it."

"Oh, come off it, Binnie," Margie Thompson, another blonde, said wearily. "If we wanted to, we could all get mad at each other. You started shacking up with Marty while I was in New York and took over my job. And I pulled the same silly stunt with Alice, who edged out Margie. Let's face it, that's the pattern. Marty gave us a big build-up and then the whole red carpet treatment, including the job as featured singer, the hoopla in the trade press and the swanky apartment. I suppose you got all that, too, Lois?"

"With a Thunderbird thrown in for good luck," Lois said irritably. "And I fell for the whole pitch."

"We all did, Honey," Mavis said. "All of us came to town with a little experience and a lot of crust. We were going to hit the big leagues in show business. We were ripe for a guy like Marty. If it hadn't been him, it would've been someone else. That's how call girls are made in Hollywood, sweetie."

"You mean he pulled the same routine with all of you?" Lois asked, surprised. "I thought he was smarter than that."

"It wasn't exactly the same routine," Mavis said. "Marty had me live with a couple of guys instead of setting me up with visiting firemen. And Margie thought she was taking on Marty's friends so he could pull some big deals and marry her. But the end result was the same. We all ended up in hock to the old maestro of the Sunset Strip. The job lasted just long enough to let him sink his hooks into us. When we got to the point where we couldn't leave, we had to move out so the next girl could move in."

"That's disgusting," Lois said.

Alice shrugged. "It's a living, if you can call it that. Anyway, you could always depend on a nice cozy party like this. Sometimes, they're held at somebody's mountain lodge or beach house. I went to an orgy at a place near Malibu about a month ago. Marty had rounded up twelve girls for fifteen guys; having fewer girls always makes it more competitive, and sometimes some of the guys just like to watch. A hundred bucks a night, plus bonuses for whatever you made some poor jerk say while a tape recorder was going. I suppose you got initiated into the tape recording bit?"

Lois nodded.

"What Marty likes best," the girl went on, thoughtfully, "is when some poor jerk asks you to do something really naughty, the kind of thing that belongs in the minority department of the Kinsey Report. If he doesn't ask you, you put the words in his mouth. Oh, Marty's a clever one; there isn't much that gets by him."

"Why do you do it?" Lois said, annoyed. "I told him I'd have no part of helping him blackmailing these men. I'm not going to, and that bastard can't make me."

"Listen, honey," Margie Thompson said patiently, "I don't know how deep this boy Marty's got his mitts into *you,* but he owns *me* lock, stock and barrel. I had to borrow a lot of money from him when my dad got sick, and all these other kids owe him a lot, too. He always makes you sign notes, and you never get enough ahead to pay him back. You get so you're glad these special projects come along, because it soon becomes a matter of survival. As far as I'm concerned, these bastards deserve what they get."

"You get realistic about it after a while," Mavis pointed out. "After you've been working for Marty for a while you're spoiled for anything else. Hell, none of us wanted to be call girls. I left

Marty and tried doing something else and nearly went out of my mind. I got a job as a secretary for some jerk in the textile line. For eighty bucks a week I was supposed to not only type his junk but sleep with him when his wife was away. I lasted a month and then begged Marty to set me up with big dates."

"It's not bad when you get used to it," Alice said. "Unless you meet a sadistic bastard like Night, they treat you pretty nice, and they pay well. Oh, you run into some weirdos once in a while who want you to duplicate some wild stuff they learned overseas, but Marty doesn't get too many of those. Mostly, they're just plain ordinary guys who want the regular thing."

One of the stewards came in. "Excuse me, ladies," he said. "Mr. Masters would like all of you to come to his cabin."

When the steward left, Mavis said, "He wants to get our tapes."

The girls rose and started filing out, until only Lois and Harriet remained seated.

Binnie paused at the doorway. "Aren't you coming?"

"In a minute," Lois said. "I want to talk to Harriet."

Binnie snorted. "Not that it means a damn to me, but maybe you ought to know something. In case you haven't heard, Marty's already asked little Harriet to take singing lessons as soon as she gets back to dry land. Your days are numbered, sweetie."

With that, Binnie flounced off triumphantly.

Lois said, "Is that true, Harriet? Did Marty say that?"

Harriet studied the table in front of her. "Yes," she said quietly.

"And he told you that you could have my spot?"

"He didn't say that," Harriet said defensively. "He just said he thought I had a pleasant voice, and that you might be leaving for—"

"Don't fall for that line, Harriet. You heard them yourself"

"Heard what?" Harriet said, flaring suddenly. "Marty warned me you'd all sharpen your knives and go after him when he wasn't around. He told me it's his policy to use new talent often and that the girls who are replaced always act like sore losers, as though they have lifetime contracts in that particular job."

For a moment, Lois' astonishment left her speechless. "But you heard them—Mavis, Margie, Alice! You heard what a double-crossing bastard he is!"

"I noticed that didn't stop *you* from taking Binnie's place," Harriet said defiantly. She rose. "I think we'd better go. Marty's waiting for us."

Lois stared at her. "I'm not going, Harriet, and if you go you're a bigger fool than I was. In my case, at least, nobody warned me about the rotten things Marty was doing."

Harriet's jaw stood out as she tightened her lips. "Do as you please. I'm sick of listening to lectures from people who muffed their chance and then blame the person who gave it to them."

Angrily, she strode from the room. Lois looked at the empty doorway and sighed. She wondered if *she* would have listened to reason if somebody had warned her about Marty when she was first starting out. Harriet would just have to learn from bitter experience, just like everyone else.

But as far as *she* was concerned, she was through being Marty's slave. The first stop was La Paz, the next day, and she would leave the ship. When she saw Marty, she'd tell him that to his face.

She didn't have to wait long to tell him. A half hour later he was pounding at her door, and when he came inside she could see he was seething.

"What the hell are you trying to do, kid?" he wanted to know. "Promote a mutiny?"

She didn't say anything.

"Let me hear what you put on tape last night," he barked at her.

"I didn't put anything on tape," she said. "I had hardly enough time to defend myself from your sadistic friend, Keene, but I wouldn't have done it anyway, even to him. I told you I wouldn't help you blackmail anyone. Maybe you weren't listening."

He stared at her as though unable to believe what she was telling him. "Maybe *you* weren't listening," he said slowly, in carefully measured tones, "so I'll tell you again, and this will be the last time. Every time you hit the sack with a guy, I want that tape recorder going. If nothing usable is said, that's not your fault. But I want the recorder going. Listen good, because I won't tell you again."

"I made no deal to blackmail anyone, damn you!" she said. "I agreed to come on as a call girl. But since you insist on that tape job, I'm quitting. As of now, I'll get off at the next port, and you can do anything you damned please. I should have had my head examined when I took you up in the first place. All that baloney about making me a show business personality and getting me roles! You never had any plans to do anything but turn me into a high-priced call girl, just like you did with every other girl on the boat."

"Nobody twisted your arm, kid," he said. "I gave you Binnie's spot—"

"Which you're handing over to little Harriet," she retorted. "Plus, I'm sure, a new car and clothes and the kind of apartment all hundred-dollar whores should have!"

Marty laughed. "So that's what's bothering you. You're insecure. You think I'm giving your job away. Look, kid, it's a matter of self-preservation. You're a rebel, a girl with more spirit than is good for you, and so you're also a troublemaker. I've got to have somebody warming up in the bull pen to take over if you just walk out, like you're threatening to do now. Don't worry about it. If you only play along, you've got your old job back at the Boomerang, with a nice long contract."

"Oh, I don't give a damn about the job," she said irritably. "When I said I was quitting, I meant all the way down the line. I'm not excluding anything. I'll get a job somewhere and pay you whatever I owe you."

His smile had drained from his face as she talked. Suddenly he grasped her arm, gripping it so roughly that she winced with pain. He pushed his face close to hers.

"You're starting to push your luck, kid. Don't do it. Don't make me do something I don't want to do. You made a deal. Stick to it. You're seeing Ducatti tonight. Be sure the recorder's running. That tape had better have some very interesting dialogue on it, or you might find yourself with every bone in your face smashed."

"You wouldn't do that," she said, unconvinced. She was remembering what Johnny had told her about Marty, about how he had arranged accidents, been involved in all sorts of underworld activities. She winced as Marty applied pressure to her arm. "Please let go. You're hurting me."

"Good," Marty said, his face twisted into a grimace. He bent her arm some more. "Maybe a broken arm might change your perspective."

"Don't, Marty, for God's sakes," she gasped as the pain shot through her arm. She could feel tears start to well up in her eyes, and she fought them back.

He loosened his grip, but the expression on his face, the intense look of hatred on it, frightened her almost as much as the twisting of her arm.

"Don't make me mad, kid," he said, his voice a hoarse whisper. "I don't like to rough somebody up or kill anybody, especially a good-looking dame, but ..."

He let the sentence trail off, but the look on his face was enough to finish it. She realized he meant it, and that he would maim or kill her if she rebelled. His business dealings were the most important things in the world to Marty. It was his life, his very existence, and Marty meant to survive at the expense of anyone who stood in his way. For the first time, she was truly terrified of him.

"Let me go," she said. "Please, Marty."

"Are you going to play my way?"

She closed her eyes and nodded slowly.

He gave her arm a twist and her eyes jerked open.

"Are you going to use that tape on Ducatti?"

She nodded, quickly this time.

Marty released her, and she stood rubbing awareness back into her arm.

"Ducatti expects you in his cabin right after dinner. God help you if you cross me on this one. You'd better have that tape filled with interesting questions and answers. And I want your voice on it, too. Is that clear? You know too much to walk a tightrope on this project, and I want you directly involved, just in case you ever think of telling anyone. I want you asking some pretty direct sex questions. Understand me?"

"Yes," Lois said, subdued.

"Okay," he said satisfied. His glacial smile returned. "You can take it easy this afternoon. But be sure you go to Ducatti's right after dinner. It won't be long. He usually poops out about midnight."

"All right," she said.

She wished he would go and leave her alone. Her arm still ached terribly, but she didn't want him to know it.

His eyes roamed up and down her body clad in the shorts and halter. "You've got a couple of nasty bruises," he said softly. "Looks like Night really went for you." He paused. "First, he asked me for Harriet. But I told him to try you. I said you'd stand up to him, and it looks like you did. But don't try it with me, kid. Not unless you want to be found floating over the side."

"All right, Marty," she said.

He turned to go, turned at the door. "You'll be through with Ducatti by midnight if he follows his usual pattern. I'll meet you in your cabin at twelve-thirty, one o'clock at the latest, with that tape. And it better be good, kid, if you value your life!"

CHAPTER FIFTEEN

The interview with Marty left Lois so shaken that she stayed in her cabin all day. Any semblance to a pleasant sea voyage had vanished, and what could have been a holiday jaunt had become an ocean-borne night-mare. Marty hadn't been idly threatening her; he'd meant every word of what he'd do if she didn't tape the rest of her sessions on board.

Once again, life had become a matter of survival, and she wondered at how easily she had gotten her life in such a hideous mess. If only she had met Elliot sooner and he'd warned her then about the dangers ahead.

She hadn't thought much about Elliot since that day he'd called upon her, but he'd been lurking in the fringes of her thoughts constantly. He'd been hurt and angry and bewildered, and she didn't really blame him for reacting as he had. He'd loved her, and this had made his discovery all the worse.

Not that it mattered any more. After what had happened, Elliot would never want to see her again. As far as he was concerned, she had reached the point of no return. And now only survival mattered.

The strong feeling of guilt persisted as she took the tiny tape recorder with her, hidden in her purse, when she went to Zundapp Ducatti's cabin that evening. It was blackmail, but she had no choice. It was either put Ducatti in Marty's power, or have Marty maim or injure her. She had nothing against Ducatti; if she had, her task would be so much easier. On the contrary, he seemed to be one of the nicest men on board. But she couldn't protect him at the risk of being pushed overboard, or worse.

Ducatti greeted her effusively when she came in. The European had ordered a magnificent array of hors d'ouevres and champagne, as well as a lavish display of fresh flowers. His approval of her tight-fitting cocktail sheath was obvious.

"You look pale, my sweet," he said solicitously. "You are not feeling seasick, I trust?"

"No," she smiled, placing her recorder-weighted purse on the bureau. "I—I'm just tired, that's all."

He grinned understanding and sympathy. "Yes, I imagine you would be tired after Mr. Keene. One of the other girls told me about him. He treats a woman like—what do they call them— sparring partners. Beats them with his fists."

"Yes, and he doesn't use the Marquis of Queensberry rules when he does it."

The sight of the trays of food reminded her that she hadn't eaten. She made herself a sandwich of smoked salmon and cream cheese on rye and wolfed it down, following it with some champagne. Watching her, Ducatti laughed in a way that made her laugh, too. There was something contagious about the good spirits of the round-faced European.

"Do you think one tray will be enough?" he asked. "Or shall I ask for more?"

"No," she laughed. "One more sandwich will do it. Where did you learn to eat combinations like this?"

"In Budapest," he said, smiling his pleasure. "It's my favorite midnight snack. You like it?"

"Mmm, wonderful. What are you anyway, Italian or German? It's hard to tell from your accent."

"Actually, I'm a Hungarian," he said, pouring himself a glass of champagne and refilling hers. "My stepfather was an Italian businessman, and I took his last name. Yes, the accent confuses everyone, as does the name." He paused and said suddenly, "You know what would please me now, very much?"

She gulped down the food in her mouth and smiled wanly. "You want me to undress."

"Oh, good heavens, not quite so fast as all that," he protested with a disarming laugh. "We have all night. No, no. I was thinking I would love dancing with you again, now that we're in no danger of interruption. That is, if you are not too tired."

"Here?" she asked, surprised by the unusual request "Of course, but there isn't any music."

He held up a forefinger and moved to a corner of the cabin to a large case that resembled a typewriter. He picked it up and put it on the table, moving her purse to one side. His gesture frightened her. She was sure he must have noticed how heavy her purse was. But he said nothing about it.

"This is a phonograph I brought back from my last trip to Berlin. Wait till you hear it."

A moment later the room was flooded with dance music. Ducatti took her in his arms and whirled her around the floor. As they danced, he kissed her several times and when it was over led her to a small sofa. She submitted to his caresses stiffly, tensely, hating every second of it, unable to respond in any way. Only her strong self-control kept her from showing her revulsion.

Ducatti frowned. "What is the trouble, Lois?" he asked quietly. "I feel as though I am making love to a statue. What is it? Am I repulsive to you? Are you afraid I am another Night Keene?"

Suddenly, she broke down and began to sob. He put her head on his shoulder and then gave her his handkerchief.

"Suppose you tell me what is wrong," he said feelingly.

Slowly, between sobs, she blurted out the whole story—Marty's instructions to tape intimate dialogues aboard ship and the rest of it.

Ducatti listened incredulously and then jumped to his feet in anger. "But this is unbelievable!" he exclaimed. "We are all hard-headed businessmen. We would beat each other out of a deal but it would always be by offering a better one, not by using young girls to record moments of intimacy—when a man is not himself and liable to talk too much."

Lois felt the sympathy she needed so badly and the tears poured forth again.

"And you mean to say," he went on, "that you girls are forced into this?"

She nodded, unable to talk.

Ducatti turned away from her, took an agitated turn around the room and returned to her, his face suddenly old and tired. "The dirty rat!" he said, his voice almost a snarl.

Then, his face softening, he dropped to his knees before Lois. "Forgive me, my dear," he murmured. "I had no idea. To tell you the truth, I never had much stomach for women bought and paid for, but when a man gets old he likes to kid himself—even if 'way down deep he knows better—that the girl bought for him is responding to him because he's dynamic and worldly—" He stopped short, shook his head sadly and muttered, half to himself, "There's no fool like an old fool."

Lois' hand came up involuntarily and stroked his cheek gently.

He patted her hand reassuringly. "Thank you for telling me, darling." With a deep sigh he got to his feet. "The others are crude men at times and they can get a little rough but I don't think they're going to like what I have to tell them."

"But I'm afraid of what Marty will do to me," Lois said worriedly through her sniffles.

"Don't worry about that," Ducatti said firmly. "I will get you off the boat before he knows what's going on. The sonofabitch! Asking girls to come along as a business deal is one thing. Forcing them is something else. I will be damned before I have anything more to do with the bastard! And I think that's how the others will feel, too!"

At eight o'clock the next morning, Marty knocked impatiently at Lois' door. Half the night he'd waited for her to come to his cabin, afraid to bust in on Ducatti and Lois for fear that the European would resent his intrusion. Tired, frustrated, he'd finally fallen into a tired sleep until he'd come to with a start, aware that something was wrong.

"Open up, damn you," he shouted.

There was no answer. He knocked several times angrily.

"Lois," he bellowed. "Get up!"

"Marty," a voice shouted behind him, and he whirled to face Binnie. "They're all leaving the ship," she went on distractedly. "All of the men. Bags and all."

"What?" Marty said incredulously. "But why?"

"Lois told Ducatti everything, and Ducatti told the men."

He cursed volubly and pushed her aside. Racing above decks, he saw the launch speeding away from the ship with its cargo of passengers.

As he stared in helpless rage, Marty wanted to kill Lois. The only thing that seemed to matter now was to get back at her no matter what it cost. In one night, she had shot the most lucrative side of his business to hell. He intercepted one of the sailors who was passing and ordered him to get the dinghy ready. Then he went to his stateroom.

"Don't worry," he said to Binnie. "I'll get that double-crossing bitch if it's the last thing I do."

He took a wad of bills from his pocket, peeled off a half dozen of them and gave them to Binnie. "I'm going after them. Hang on to this in case you or the girls need transportation."

He went to the bureau and removed a gun from under a pile of shirts. He made sure it was loaded, and then he shoved it in his pocket.

A half-hour later, as a plane was taxiing off the field, Marty entered the airport office of the La Paz airfield. He held out a photograph of Lois to the man behind the counter.

"Anyone like this leave here?"

The Mexican examined the photograph carefully and nodded. "She left with a man on the eight-thirty plane to Tijuana, señor." He waved a hand toward the airplane roaring down the runway. "That one."

Marty cursed under his breath. "When's the next flight?"

"There is none until four o'clock this afternoon," the Mexican said sadly.

Marty held out a roll of bills. "I want to leave right away," he said.

The Mexican's face broke into a grin. "Charters are available, sir."

Within ten minutes, Marty was sitting in the seat behind the pilot of a light, closed plane, and the Mexican terrain was flashing below them. He felt his nerves tense in anticipation of catching the girl who had dared double-cross him. He tried to relax and couldn't. He hated Lois too much. She had ruined everything for him, just by opening her big mouth. He could never do business again with any of the men who had been on board the Greyhound, and probably with any of their friends. Word got around fast.

But there was still a chance. A slim one, but the only one he had. He could say that Zundapp had been lying, that it had been a trick to steal Lois away. And only Zundapp or Lois could say that it was the truth—if they were alive.

Marty smiled and patted the reassuring weight of the loaded gun in his coat pocket. It would be pleasant seeing the two of them again. It was more than even the need for survival. There was a score that had to be settled, once and for all.

CHAPTER SIXTEEN

Zundapp Ducatti and Lois relaxed as soon as they reached Tijuana and alighted casually with the planeload of California fishermen from La Paz. After customs was done with, they went to a bar for a drink and lunch. Ducatti was not one to fear any man and Lois felt completely secure in his company.

"You're not likely to get your old job back at the Boomerang Club," Zundapp pointed out to her. "What are your plans, Lois?"

She stared at her drink and then sipped it thoughtfully. "I don't know Zundapp, I honestly don't."

"I would like to have you reconsider my offer," he said. "Marty will not rest until he exacts his revenge. I know his type. I can set you up in an apartment and have a bodyguard watch over you. You will be safe."

She smiled gratefully and placed a hand on his arm. "Thanks very much. Zundapp. You're one of the nicest people I've ever known, and if I wanted to be the mistress of anybody it would be you. But—"

"But there is someone else?" he suggested.

She nodded and thought of Elliot. She wondered what he was doing now, and who he was with, and if he ever thought of her. If he did ever think of her any more, she hoped it would be kindly, remembering the many good memories, forgetting the bad ones. She didn't think it was too much to ask.

It was late at night when they walked through the crowded neon streets of Tijuana toward the border.

"A kind of Mexican Coney Island," Ducatti said pleasantly. "I've been here a few times when I've gone to Mexico City from Los Angeles. I don't care much for it—the commercialism."

On the American side, they went to a car rental place, and Zundapp selected a late model Pontiac. They drove it onto the express highway leading from the border to San Diego, merging with the evening traffic carrying scores of American tourists from the honky-tonks and bargain shops of the Mexican border town.

"Zundapp!" Lois cried in sudden alarm, taking his arm.

"What is it?"

"That car that just passed us. I could swear it was Marty driving."

Zundapp's eyes narrowed thoughtfully. "Marty could have chartered a plane to get him to Tijuana, but how could he find us in all this traffic?"

"He could have checked the car rental places," she suggested, "until he found out the one we used."

"Which means he could also find out from the rental agency the kind of car we have and our license number," Zundapp said darkly. "I don't wish to alarm you, my dear, but we may be in for trouble."

The car ahead of them was a late model Cadillac. Marty would have chosen a high horsepower car in an effort to catch them. The driver of the car was holding back, glancing in his rear-view mirror.

"I—I think he's recognized us," Lois said, panic edging into her voice.

"I am afraid you're right," Ducatti agreed sadly. "I don't know if Marty would do anything on the freeway. I suspect he would though. If he could get us to crash, it would cause a tieup and he could get away without anyone knowing. Our only chance is to run for it."

His foot tromped on the accelerator and, in answer, the Pontiac leaped forward. They swung into the far left lane, passing cars, and then proceeded to weave in and out of the slower traffic. Lois glanced back at the black Cadillac, watching it move from one lane to another, maneuvering to keep up with them.

"It *is* Marty!" she said.

Zundapp merely nodded, keeping his eyes on the road ahead, where the bright lights of the Pontiac punched brilliant cones in the night. The traffic around them was thinning as they passed the slower-moving vehicles. When they reached a stretch of open road, the speedometer read ninety-five. Behind them, Marty's car burst free of the traffic and accelerated after them.

"He's catching up!" Lois said.

"I am doing all I can," Zundapp said helplessly.

Lois watched in horrified fascination as the huge black Cadillac slowly crept up on them, closing the gap steadily. When he was a car length behind, Marty edged his car over into the right lane, and then slowly began moving alongside them.

In unison, as though held together by a slowly shrinking wire, the two cars hurtled down the dark road. The speedometer read one hundred now, and Lois closed her eyes, listening to the whistling of the wind past the window, the giant roar of the engine, the whir of the tires, and she prayed that beyond the next curve there would be no traffic. At this speed, if they ran into something—

She looked up and out of the car window and she gasped as she saw the black Cadillac moving directly alongside and Marty's face just a few yards from her, his features triumphant and livid with rage. His hand appeared at the window sill of his car holding an ugly black pistol.

"He's got a gun!" Lois cried.

Ducatti glanced over. "He is a madman. Hold on, my dear!"

He pulled at the steering wheel and the Pontiac jerked over toward the right lane. There was a crash, the sound of grinding metal. The two cars bounced apart; Lois was thrown sideways on the seat beside Ducatti. She felt the rear of the car start to slide, felt Ducatti struggling frantically to correct the course of it.

She rose in the seat and looked out. The Cadillac was still beside them, its side dented from the impact. It was swerving crazily, shooting ahead of them for a moment, then running off the side of the road.

She caught a fleeting glimpse of the Cadillac again as it turned over, rolling once, twice. Then the Pontiac spun and she hung on to the edge of the seat. Her eyes went wide with fear and she caught brief glimpses of the oncoming traffic, a giant wall of rock, traffic signs, guard rails held by white metal posts that resembled cemetery tombstones.

The world spun crazily, and then it stopped as they hit a signpost, and Lois found herself hurtling like a bullet toward the windshield ...

CHAPTER SEVENTEEN

The world was a dark place for a long time and then, slowly, consciousness returned. It brought pain with it, a headache such as none Lois had ever known. She forced her eyes open against the glare of light, focusing them on the patterns reflected onto the ceiling. She was in a bed in a hospital room and a nurse was standing nearby looking at her chart. Lois recalled the chase, Marty pulling alongside, Zundapp crashing into the other car in self-defense.

"Where am I?" she asked.

"San Diego General Hospital," the nurse said, smiling at her. "How do you feel?"

"I have a headache," Lois said.

"I shouldn't wonder. You'll have a lot of other aches when the sedation wears off completely. You were lucky, though. A slight concussion, lots of bruises, but nothing serious."

"Mr. Ducatti, the man I was with—?"

"Fine. He's got a broken arm and some bruises, but other than that he's all right."

Lois relaxed between the cool sheets and breathed a sigh of relief. Awareness crapt back upon her, and she could feel the bandages on her head, the soreness blossoming throughout her body.

"There's someone outside to see you," the nurse said. "Doctor says it's all right if you feel up to it."

Lois nodded, wondering who it could be. A moment later, she found out.

"Johnny!" she cried delightedly.

Johnny Kay had a bouquet of roses in his hand. He stood beside her and awkwardly brushed a lock of hair from his forehead. "How are you, honey?" he said, bending over to kiss her. "The things a girl will do for publicity! You'll be glad to know you made the front page of every paper in L.A."

"Johnny, what happened to Marty?" Lois asked slowly.

"He—he was killed instantly," Johnny said. "But I checked with the doc, and he says you'll be okay. In fact, you'll be out in about a week." He laughed shyly. "I—uh—I'm staying at a motel about a half mile from here. I figured I ought to be here when you need me."

Her heart leaped with the knowledge that someone cared. She gave him a wan, grateful smile. "But what about your job?"

"Club's shut down," he said. "Nobody's working."

She'd been so glad to see him she hadn't noticed that he'd been drinking. Now Lois saw his shaking hands, his bloodshot eyes—there was no doubt about it, he'd had a snootful.

"Listen, Lois, I've got an idea," he slurred. "I've been thinking about it all day. There's no point in either of us hanging around L.A. I talked to my agent and he says he can book us both into a place in Chicago for almost the same money we got from Marty."

She shook her head. "I don't want to think about anything like that now, Johnny."

"There's no hurry, honey," he said. "I just wanted to mention it to you. The agent said he'd wait until you got out of the hospital. Then maybe we can drive out there in your car."

He took a piece of paper from his wallet. "I brought your check. The accountant made them out before Marty was killed. You had two weeks' pay coming."

"Thanks, Johnny. Put it on the table, will you?"

He cleared his throat awkwardly. "I hate to ask you, Lois, but could you let me have about three hundred of it? I'll get it back to you as soon as I can."

"Three hundred dollars?" she said, distressed. "Johnny, I'm going to need all that money. Didn't you get a check, too?"

"Sure, I did," he said petulantly. "But by the time I pay people off, I'll be broke."

"I'm sorry, Johnny," she said feelingly. "But I'm going to need—"

"Look, it's your fault we're in this pickle," he complained. "If you hadn't crossed Marty, we wouldn't have closed down. We wouldn't both be out on our cans. And just when I needed every cent I could lay my hands on."

"You'll find something, Johnny," she said.

"It's easy for you to talk," he almost whimpered. "With looks like yours you can always get along. Why the hell couldn't you go along with the deal, for Pete's sake? Would it have been so terrible to put up with it for another few weeks, instead of knocking the props out from under both of us?"

She closed her eyes as he continued to whine and her heart went out to him. For a moment she thought of giving him the money he had asked for, then she realized it wouldn't do any good. She'd only be depriving herself, forcing herself into a corner again, and Johnny would never change. He was weak—much weaker even then she had been—a leech, a barnacle.

She remembered all the pity she had wasted on him, giving him money she could ill afford to part with, the giving of which had forced her deeper and deeper into situations she'd wanted no part of.

Well, if she was to start a new life, now was the time to do it. What she needed was a break from the past—a quick, deft surgeon's cut.

She opened her eyes. Johnny hadn't moved. He was still looking at her with that familiar woebegone look of a stray, hungry cat, his tongue licking his lips in anticipation of a handout.

My God, she thought. *He never really gave a damn about me—not even as a friend. I was just someone to be used.* Her mind revolted at the truth. *He's no better than Marty was. All he wants is money and he doesn't care how I make it.*

Johnny's quavering voice cut through her thoughts. "Lois … ?" he begged

She steeled herself against the pleading of his voice and eyes. "Get out, Johnny," she said quietly.

"Wha—?"

"I don't want to see you again," she added quickly.

At first he stared unbelievingly, then he found his voice. "Fine thing," he whimpered. "You get me into this mess, blow everything sky-high—"

His complaint ended on a high sputter as Lois deliberately turned her back on him and the nurse stepped into the room to announce that he had to leave, that he was upsetting her patient.

Johnny, his mouth agape with bewilderment and frustration, turned and bolted from the room, leaving a trail of unintelligible, meaningless sounds. The nurse patted Lois' shoulder reassuringly and left the room.

There was soothing, welcome silence again. Except that with it came disturbing thoughts. What was she going to do now? Where would she go?

Not back to the Boomerang, even under a new management, nor to any other club where she'd be back in the same old rat race. Not home to St. Louis, because that wasn't home, never had been and never could be, especially now. Chicago? New York? Perhaps. Or some small town where she could live peacefully and try to forget the things that had happened and the things that could have been.

She tossed and turned for what seemed like hours, going over and over the same ground, trying to find a way out, endeavoring to catch a clear picture of that new life she had so bravely promised herself. At some point the nurse had come in again and found her bathed in cold sweat from head to toe.

With kindness and understanding she had given Lois a cooling sponge bath, changed the bed linen and, with the same reassuring pat, had left the room. And Lois, somewhat refreshed now, saw the turmoil for what it was: a violent reaction to the first definite step she had taken toward a new life. Johnny had been neurotically dependent on her, that was true, but she had also been neurotically dependent on him. It had been that crying need for being needed …

Suddenly, clearly, she knew what had to be done. She would get a job—any job—and go to secretarial school at night. Singing was out. Unless she ever got to the point where she could sing for the sheer joy of singing, instead of to quiet the sick, driving thirst for approval and admiration. Would that day ever come? She didn't know. She didn't care.

Into this new calmness came a voice, calling her name, and she blinked in disbelief and then inclined her head to look toward the end of the bed Her heart raced.

"Elliot!" she said, wondering if this was some mirage that might vanish at any instant. "Elliot!"

"Don't talk, darling," he said, moving toward her as she started to rise, "and lie back and rest. The nurse told me I've only got a couple of minutes—that you've been too upset."

"Oh, not any more!" she insisted. "Not any more!"

He took a deep breath. "I've been out of my mind with worry ever since you disappeared. Then I read about it in the papers and got sick thinking of the way I'd treated you."

"Elliot—"

"No, just listen. I'm not going into a song and dance about what happened. I was hurt and angry, and I just lashed out at you. When I simmered down later, I realized that you'd been trapped and that you'd been trying to break out. The point is, you'd already seen your mistake—"

He paused, carefully forming his next words. Lois gazed at him for a moment, not speaking, letting her eyes recall the details of his face that she was afraid she would never see again.

"I love you, Lois," he said quietly. "If you'll have me, I'd like to marry you."

Her vision became blurred by sudden tears and she shook her head.

"It's no use, Elliot. Thanks. But it wouldn't work. You couldn't help remembering. And just when we both got to thinking the past was dead and buried, we might run into someone who knew me *when* and it would start all over again. You'd never be sure someone wouldn't try to hire me for the night—"

"Honey, I know it's not going to be easy, but I'm willing to try. Are you?"

"But—"

"I think we've got a lot of pluses going for us and it's worth a try." He bent down and blocked further protest with his lips. For a second she resisted, but the tenderness, the warmth and sincerity of him overwhelmed her, and her arms crept up over his back and pulled him closer to her while her lips worked against his, fervently, passionately.

He broke away and straightened. "I'll be staying at the El Cortez Hotel until you get out of the hospital. Then I'll take you home."

There was something about the way he said it that made her know home would be wherever Elliot was.

"All right—darling," she said.

He took her hand. "Hurry and get well," he said. "We've got a lot of things to do together."

"I will," she promised. "I will, Elliot."

Then he was gone, but thoughts of him persisted. She loved him very much and because she did she would do everything in her power to make a go of their marriage. And, together, they would succeed. They had to. There would be times when it wouldn't be easy, but she felt a sudden elation at the opportunity presented her and felt happiness and determination flooding her.

She relaxed on the bed, firm in her decision. Yes, she and Elliot would try and, what's more, they would succeed, because now she knew what life was all about. It was loving—one man— and giving only that one man the right to ask for Lois.

THE END